BACK TO SALEM

A TIME TRAVEL ROMANCE

LOVE THROUGHOUT TIME
BOOK SEVEN

ID JOHNSON

For Ashlee. Glad you're still here.

CONTENTS

FOOTSTEPS OF THE ACCUSED

LILA

THE STAGE LIGHTS DIM, LEAVING ONLY THE RICOCHET OF FOOTSTEPS and lines reverberating in the rafters. My palms are damp as I smooth the coarse fabric of Martha Carrier's plain dress, still hoping to calm the butterflies fluttering in my stomach. *This is only a rehearsal,* I remind myself. Yet, standing here in the stiff collar and bonnet, I feel something more than performance. Martha's defiant words linger like a bitter taste in my mouth.

"Which of you have I wronged?" I had shouted just minutes ago, emotion carrying across the auditorium. For a moment, I wasn't myself anymore. I was her: exhausted, furious, and unyielding. I was the so-called Queen of Hell, the one who would not bend, not even with a rope tightening around her neck.

The director calls, "That's it for tonight." His words break the spell.

The others laugh and chatter as they peel away their costumes, but I move slower, reluctant to shed Martha's persona. I tug at the ties beneath my chin and slide the bonnet free. My curls tumble down, sticking to the sweat at my temples. Tonight I'm too tired to change clothes here, so I'll wait until I get home, strip off these layers, and let the hot water of a steamy shower wash the day away.

Jenna strides over, her apron half off, and stops beside me. "Lila, seriously," she says. "The way you cry when Madison acts like she slaps you—I got chills! You really made me believe she slapped your face."

I manage a tired chuckle. "Thanks, Jenna. I've always liked the physical part of acting. I just try to imagine what Martha was going through."

"Well, it works," Jenna says. "Even Joanne and Miles were watching you. They've never been that impressed in rehearsal."

I glance toward the group of seasoned actors. Each of them brings their own perspective to the story. Joanne's Rebecca Nurse is quiet and unnerving in her calm, while Miles's John Proctor practically bursts with fury every time he speaks. They make history come alive on stage. And Jenna is doing a wonderful job playing Mary English, a wealthy woman who was accused of witchcraft but later escaped Salem.

"I'm just happy I was chosen again this year. Last year I played 'Village Woman,' so having a speaking role has been quite the upgrade." I smile.

"You're going to make people remember Martha for her heart and fire, not just the trial," Jenna replies. "Don't lose that edge, and that courage she had when she faced them all."

I nod, letting her words settle, grateful for the reminder of why I love acting, why I endure the long practices and stiff costumes to step out there and bring these stories back from the scaffold.

"We're sticking around for a bit, ordering takeout, going over lines one more time. You should stay. Hang out with us a little longer?" Jenna pleads.

I shake my head, rubbing my temples. "I wish I could, but I'm wiped. It's been a long day, and I have class early in the morning. Thanks for offering, though."

Her smile softens with understanding, and she claps a hand briefly on my arm. "Fair enough. Don't let me guilt you. Just know we'll be here if you change your mind."

"Thanks, Jenna. I'll see you tomorrow."

When I step outside, the cold breeze smacks me awake. February in Massachusetts doesn't play gentle. The pavement glistens with frost, street lamps haloing pale light over the brick facades.

I walk slowly, my bag thumping against my hip, exhaustion tugging at my limbs. This afternoon I was buried under case files at the firm, paralegal drudgery that chews through my soul one stapled packet at a time. Tomorrow I'll drag myself to the lecture hall, highlight rules of evidence until my eyes cross, and pretend I don't hear the nagging in my head asking what the hell I'm doing with my life. I'd so much rather be practicing law already and defending people who are innocent instead of being in class all morning and working for corporate lawyers all evening. But here at the theater, I feel a sliver of freedom.

Unlike Martha, who lost everything–her home, her dignity, her life–and still she refused to admit to lies, even to the very end. I can't shake that. I've been haunted by foster homes, by the way adults scowled at me and judged me like I was already broken, when I was just a child.

My parents died in a car accident when I was ten, and I was shuffled around like a problem no one wanted to keep. I learned early on in life that silence keeps you out of trouble, but Martha chose the opposite. She raised her voice until history couldn't forget it.

The lines from rehearsal remain vivid in my mind, and I feel as though I am still rehearsing, speaking for women who were silenced in the most brutal of ways. Salem lore has always had this effect on me, blending the boundary between history and imagination until both feel inseparable, and I am left walking in the footsteps of the accused even as I return to my ordinary life.

I have known these stories for as long as I can remember, woven into the fabric of the town where I grew up. Children here don't learn fairy tales first. We're raised on accounts of trials and executions, on whispered tales about spirits and witches, on the quiet dread that never seems to fade from the soil itself.

Those stories made their home inside me, and with them grew a fascination that set me apart. I wanted to know all things witchcraft, so I learned to recognize herbs by sight and name, to recall their uses without needing to check a book, to brew teas and tinctures that seem harmless today, but once carried suspicion heavy enough to destroy lives.

The costume I'm still wearing suddenly feels absurd here in the parking lot full of cars. Luckily, no one else is around. I grip my keys tightly, the frozen metal digging into my palm as I walk between rows of vehicles gleaming with a brittle sheen of frost.

A sharp gust of wind cuts across the asphalt, stinging my eyes with tears. I don't notice the danger beneath me until it is too late. My boot strikes a patch of black ice, and in the same instant, my balance vanishes.

I lose my footing and fall violently, my keys slipping from my hand with a metallic clatter against the pavement and the stiff dress tangling around my legs. The ground rises fast, and then a sharp burst of pain explodes at the back of my skull as it meets the concrete.

For an instant, I am aware only of the cold rushing into me, bone-deep and merciless, and my eyelids dragging closed as though held down with stones. There's a ringing in my ears, and then darkness claims me completely.

When I open my eyes, I have no idea how much time has passed, and my head throbs. My body is heavy and unresponsive. Light shimmers at the edges of my vision, bright then dim, until it becomes silver, and soft like moonlight on snow.

Snow… I'm lying in a field I don't recognize. My breath puffs into tiny clouds, and the nearby crunch of boots on frozen ground sends a jolt through me.

Tall, cloaked shapes glide across the white ground. I try to speak, to demand they tell me who they are, but when I open my mouth, nothing comes out. My neck tightens sharply, a dull, sinking ache spreading from the base of my skull down to my shoulders, as if I'm feeling the pressure of those hanged. It's a paralysis that creeps through me, and I can't lift my head.

The field blurs, dissolving into the dim orange glow of parking lot lamps. Salted asphalt gleams in my peripheral vision. I'm back at the theater. Relief almost unravels me--until the darkness pours back in again.

Shapes flash: a woman standing proud with bound wrists, lanterns swinging, people being pulled from rough wooden homes. My chest tightens as my pulse slows, the echo of voices like accusations across generations.

Sparks dance, and shadows bend and twirl. I try to call out, to beg for help, but my lips refuse, and all my energy is swallowed by the freezing night.

Then briefly, I see other figures: men and women with garments stitched from animal hides, their faces painted with streaks of red and black. Their peaceful presence feels necessary, a lifeline in the dark.

I roll my head back and forth, trying to stay conscious and remember where I am, but my strength fails. I can't lift my arms, and the shapes and sounds, the ice and snow, all collapse together into one endless gray void. My last thought is of Martha Carrier, standing fearless at the gallows, before everything goes black.

CHILLED TO THE BONE

LILA

I WAKE to the sting of snow against my face, every muscle screaming in protest. My costume is soaked, sticking to me, and the cold gnaws through my gloves and boots. If I lay here much longer, I will definitely freeze to death.

Above, trees stretch upward like dark, frozen watchmen. I try focusing, but the white haze and shadowed trunks blur together.

Where in the hell am I?

I try to move, and my body protests in sharp, stabbing pain. My arms feel like lead, and my legs are heavy and uncooperative. A shiver wracks me from toes to scalp, and panic flares. The forest is silent except for the faint whistle of wind through skeletal branches. I'm completely alone.

Slowly, stubbornly, I inch an arm forward, then the other. The snow compresses beneath me as I push onto my hands and knees. Every movement sends pain lancing through my joints, but finally, I sit upright. My head spins.

I plant my feet into the icy ground, testing my balance. I rise, my knees wobbling and my chest tight with fear, and take a careful step. I'm standing. I'm moving. I have no idea where this place is, or how I got here, but I am alive.

I stumble through the snow, each step sending a shooting pain through my legs. My head pounds, my breath comes in bursts, and for a moment, I wonder if I'm even awake.

Every so often, I think I see movement between the trees, but I can't tell if it's real or my imagination. My breath puffs in clouds, and my hands are numb, gripping my frozen dress tightly.

Then I see figures stepping out from the shadows, their long, dark braids adorned with beads and feathers. They wear deerskin tunics and leggings, decorated with intricately stitched fringe that sways with each step of moccasins crunching softly on the snow. They move with a quiet precision, closing in around me almost like they'd been watching all along, encircling me before I even realize they are there.

I nearly shriek. Every cell of my body buzzes with terror. These are real people, women from a world centuries before mine, and I have no idea if they mean to help me or if I've just wandered into a danger I can't even name.

"Follow," one of them says in a calm voice. Relief floods into my veins. I nod, my legs trembling as I take a cautious step forward. The women exchange glances, then gesture again for me to keep close. I do, careful not to stumble.

They move with authority, guiding me along packed paths between thick trunks. One lifts her bundle, reaches into it, and hands me something warm. It's a fur-lined shawl, and she wraps it tightly around my neck. I grasp it and nod in gratitude.

We navigate deeper into the forest. Occasionally, one speaks a word or two in choppy English: "Fire." "Food." I nod, repeating them under my breath, clinging to any connection I can make.

At last, we reach a grove where the women kneel, gathering dry bark and twigs from beneath the evergreens and coaxing a spark into flame. They motion for me to sit near the warmth. One offers a fresh change of clothes. Mine are so frozen, I peel them off and change immediately. I can feel my body seconds away from hypothermia, and frost-bite is threatening the tips of my ears.

The women hand me dried meat and nuts, which I accept with shaking hands, marveling at their kindness. An older woman, her hair streaked silver, fans the flames, while a younger, incredibly striking woman with high cheekbones and a braided crown of dark hair lifts a small pot she carries on her belt, setting it onto the fire. Soon, the water hisses, steam rises, and the older woman drops in a handful of herbs. I recognize them as sweet fern and red raspberry leaf.

When the tea is ready, she pours it into a cup and holds it out to me. I wrap my fingers around it, the scent of herbs curling into my nose, and take a careful sip, feeling the warmth spread through my frozen limbs. Their company, the fire's crackle, and the gentle warming of the tea and the food in my belly feels like a lifeline in the endless cold, and I let myself draw strength from it.

Eventually, they rise and motion for me to follow. I push myself to my feet, my legs weak but willing. The warmth of the fire stays briefly on my skin as we leave the clearing behind, its glow swallowed by the growing dusk.

We wind through narrow, twisting trails. The women move ahead with confidence, their eyes constantly scanning the forest, their lips pressed in concentration. I try to match their pace, despite my stiff muscles and scattered thoughts. We pass gnarled branches coated in frost and ice-laden streams glinting in the weak sunlight.

Soon, more voices drift through the trees, low murmurs, along with the distant clatter of wood on wood. Smoke curls from chimneys farther ahead. My stomach knots with fear, yes, but also a spark of hope. Life exists here. People live, work, and survive here. Perhaps I'm not trapped in some endless wilderness, after all.

When we emerge from the edge of the forest into open ground, the signs are unmistakable. This is Salem. I grew up here, and even in a primitive form, I'd recognize my hometown anywhere.

One of the indigenous women glances back at me, her expression firm but gentle, and she gestures for me to keep moving. I obey, though my steps falter, each one weighed down by disbelief. I scan the buildings, noting their details.

A small girl crosses the path ahead carrying a basket, her skirts dusted with snow. She pauses, regards us with a curious expression, then continues on.

My legs ache, but I manage to keep walking. As I turn to the women who brought me this far, I choke out a "Thank you" between shivers, the words spilling out breathless and clumsy. I don't know if they understand me, but it's the only thing I can offer–gratitude, and the realization that I would have died without them.

The youngest of the group, her cheeks flushed from the cold, steps closer. She can't be much younger than me, maybe twenty, but she carries herself with the poise of someone who has endured far more than I can imagine.

"You," she begins, her eyes never leaving mine. "*Yengees*—" she gestures toward the small cluster of houses ahead. "For you." She leans closer, lowering her voice. "Stay like running stream."

She sweeps her hands in a low, flowing motion, then gestures forward, showing me to move along and keep blending in, to not linger here.

"Yengees?" I ask aloud, tilting my head toward her.

The girl points toward the people walking through the village and repeats the word, sharper this time, as if emphasizing it.

Something finally clicks in my brain. Yengees—this is what she's calling the villagers. The English.

She taps her hand against her chest. "Naya."

"Lila," I whisper back, pressing my hand to my chest in return. It feels like a fragile kind of pact, something woven in the cold dusk between two women who may never meet again.

"You," Naya says, pointing toward the forest path behind us, "follow path. Naya."

I swallow hard, my breath fogging in the icy air. "I will."

Before I can say more, the sound of voices drifts toward us– women's voices, calling to one another. A small group approaches from the village, their heavy wool skirts brushing the ground, white caps tied tight over their hair. Their steps are steady, purposeful, their eyes narrowing as they take me in.

Now that I'm no longer completely frozen, my mind has room for thought again, and the thoughts are not comforting.

What year is this? What century?

The indigenous women's clothing gives me almost no clue. I'm embarrassingly undereducated in their history, though I think these must be Naumkeag, since I remember the name attached to this region. But the village before me... it clicks too late, like a door slamming shut inside my head. Salem in its infancy.

A few village women step cautiously from the cluster of buildings, their faces a mix of confusion, curiosity, and concern. Their eyes move over the borrowed Indigenous American outfit I wear, the damp, ice-encrusted dress clutched in my hands, and the way the women beside me guide me forward, their hands pressing on my elbows, urging me closer without a word.

One of the older women, her hair streaked with gray and her posture still firm despite the years, steps ahead. Her eyes scan me quickly, taking in every detail, then shift to the indigenous women. Whispered words pass between them, a soft exchange I can't understand, and I feel the subtle nudges, the gestures urging me to move.

"Child," the village woman says, her voice calm but edged with authority. "Are you all right? You look chilled to the bone."

"I... I am cold, but I think I'll be all right," I stammer, my teeth chattering despite the warmth of the fur. "I... I was in the woods... and these kind women helped me." I glance back at the indigenous women, who nod encouragingly.

The older Puritan woman studies me a moment longer then turns toward my rescuers. "Thank you," she says, her tone full of respect and relief. "You have saved her life."

The indigenous American women exchange nods, murmuring in their own language, their hands pressed together briefly in acknowledgment.

Turning to me, the woman says, "I am Rebecca Nurse."

The name strikes me like a blow. My knees buckle, and my vision fades in and out. Rebecca Nurse, one of the most famous victims of the Salem witch hysteria.

How is she alive? How is she speaking to me?

I feel nauseated and begin to sway. Before I can collapse, Naya's hands catch me, her grip fierce. She steadies me just long enough for Rebecca and the other village women to step in.

Naya's eyes meet mine once more, full of concern, before she gently nudges me, and then I am walking forward, into Salem Village, my heart hammering with a dread I can barely contain.

FEAR BREEDS FEAR

ALEXANDER

I RISE WITH THE SUN, its pale light spilling across the frost-hardened fields of my small farm. My breath fogs the air as I step into the yard. My boots crunch over the frozen soil, and the breeze bites through my coat, but the fire of purpose and responsibility warms me. My livestock stir as I approach: a few goats, cows, chickens, a pair of hogs, and a mare, huddled in the barn.

I feed the hogs first, tossing bucketfuls of scraps into their troughs, before my younger brother Phineas appears, trudging through the snow toward me.

"Morning, Alexander," he says, his eyes twinkling with mischief.

I grin at him, shifting the bucket. "And what brings you to my farm so early, Phineas? Come to steal my breakfast before the rooster even crows?"

Phineas laughs, his cheeks red from the chill. "Better than breakfast, brother. I have gossip. There are murmurings of strange happenings. The girls, Betty Parris and Abigail Williams, continue having fits and claiming they're bewitched. They point fingers at Tituba, saying she's a witch who is making them possessed by the *devil*."

I pause, letting the words settle as I toss a handful of hay in for the goats. "Aye," I murmur, glancing toward Salem in the distance. "I've heard idle talk. These aren't ordinary rumors."

"No, Alexander," Phineas says, lowering his voice. "People say it's of Satan himself. Tituba is already the talk of the town, and the elders grow fearful. Father and Mother are unsettled, and the whole hamlet is on edge."

I shake my head, a prickle running up my spine. "Phineas, don't swallow every tale you hear. Our faith walks hand in hand with fear, and it was only a matter of time before that fear spilled over into chaos."

Phineas nods, a wry grin tugging at his lips. "Aye, brother. 'Tis the Puritan way, guiding hearts with dread and discipline, and no wonder such unease spreads through every home."

"Aye, but let's not be consumed by gossip. The day grows long, and the animals require tending."

Phineas shivers, and I pat his shoulder, not that it will warm him much. "Steady now," I tell him. "Mind your words and your steps. Salem is in an unrestful season."

Together, we begin mending a fence, hammering the post until it holds, but I'm still consumed by thoughts of tension in the town. Every face passing on the road seems shadowed by suspicion. Even neighbors once trusting have been glancing at one another sideways, weighing the chance that someone is not who they claim.

Witchcraft, they whisper, but I know it is just scandals and fear-mongering. Tituba, the Parris family's Caribbean slave, has become the focus of their accusations, as if her presence alone could stir everyone into a frenzy.

I can't help but think the girls chose her deliberately. Tituba is not like the rest of us, and I know the village will gather against anyone who stands apart. Her skin, her speech, and her origins make her easy to blame, and the children have only learned to follow the crowd.

By midmorning, winter gnaws less insistently, and Phineas and I sling our tools over our shoulders, heading down the frozen path toward our parents' house. Smoke curls lazily from the chimney, and

I can smell the faint tang of burning wood and simmering stew even before we reach the door.

Mother stands at the hearth, tending a pot, her hands busy. Father leans against the table, carving a piece of seasoned meat, his expression grave but softened by our arrival.

"Ah, my sons," Mother says, her voice calm but carrying the undercurrent of worry that never leaves Salem these days. "Come in before your noses freeze off entirely."

My brother and I step onto the worn boards, shedding our boots. The warmth of the fireplace hits immediately, and I close my eyes for a moment, savoring it.

We sit around the table, our plates and bowls soon filled with stew, bread, salted meat, and the last of the winter squash.

"Words travel fast," Father says. "I saw Martha Jacobs at the well this morning, and she's been babbling to half the village. Talk of spirits and fits." He shakes his head. "The girls in Parris's house are causing enough stir, but now everyone looks over their shoulder. Fear breeds fear."

Mother nods, handing me a hunk of bread. "I remember when Betty Parris first started screaming, rolling on the floor like she'd seen a devil. Everyone was ready to blame it on some wicked spell, but your father and I think it's nothing more than an act. Those little girls are simply trying to stir up trouble for attention's sake."

Phineas shifts, nudging his plate. "I agree, Mother, but do any of you think part of this is real?" he asks quietly. "I mean, Tituba is from an island where they practice…."

Father fixes him with a steady gaze, sharp but not angry. "You hold your tongue, Phineas Paine. Tituba is a godly, honest woman. That she comes from a distant land is no reason for idle talk or assumptions against her."

Mother passes food around to us once more. "You boys must eat," she says, clearly trying to change the subject. "Keep your strength in this cold winter…."

Father leans back, his eyes distant. "Your grandfather used to say no man is guided to virtue by threats. Punishment may silence him for a time, but it can't teach him righteousness. In the end, it breeds only turmoil."

Phineas tilts his head, his face still curious and boyish. "What does that mean?"

I inhale deeply. "It means our way of life makes folks bind themselves so tight with rules and penance that something in them pushes back. They rebel in secret, even if they never show it, and when enough souls do that all at once, the whole of society starts to crack."

Phineas turns this over in silence, his brow furrowed. The room grows quiet after my words; the only sound is the scrape of spoons against the wooden bowls.

After we finish eating, I glance at Phineas. "I'm heading to Hez's," I say. "I need to see what he's heard."

Mother frowns. "Keep warm," she warns.

I rise from the table and clasp Phineas's shoulder. "I will, Mother. Thank you for the meal," I say.

"Go well, Alexander," Mother says, her eyes warm. "We love you."

Father nods. "Mind yourself out there. Watch your step."

I glance at Phineas. "Don't get into trouble while I'm gone, Phin."

He grins, shrugging with the nonchalance of sixteen, and nods.

I pull my coat tighter and set off down the path, making my way toward Hezekiah's house on the next ridge, a narrow lane lined with picket fences and a small orchard.

Hezekiah greets me at the door, grinning. "Alexander! Come in, come in. You'll freeze out there! Listen to that wind!" He gestures to a stool by the hearth. "I've heard a dozen new prats before breakfast, some wild, all concerning."

"What's new?" I ask, shedding my coat, my fingers still stiff from the frost.

"Abigail Williams," he says, leaning closer, lowering his voice. "She had a fit at the meeting house last night, twisting and screaming like she was possessed. Screaming, "Witch!" over and over, and saying that she had a demon inside of her. And Tituba, well, people are saying the slave woman encouraged her. Some swear she was muttering incantations the entire time."

I frown, gripping the edge of the table. "All this talk of witches is quite unsettling. Makes a man wonder what else he ought to be tending to before the panic spreads." I look to my satchel. "I should fetch some herbs and supplies from the apothecary."

Hezekiah's eyes gleam. "I'll join you, friend. I never miss a chance to see the stir of the town."

We step into the snow together, the borough unfolding around us. Hezekiah chatters on, filling me in on details of yesterday's news: Mrs. Putnam scolding her children for speaking to "witchy" people, chatter about a stranger who claims to see spirits in the woods, and how Mrs. Proctor told Mrs. Parris she shouldn't believe her own daughter, causing Mrs. Parris to slap her and walk away.

At the apothecary, we wait our turn in a short line. Martha Corey leans toward her friend, Mary Porter, speaking in a hushed, hurried tone. "I swear Tituba was seen in the night, chanting. Abigail followed her like she were in a trance."

Mary gasps.

Hezekiah grabs a few items and glances at me, noticing my distraction. "Did you hear something worth repeating?" he asks, his expression far too pleased under the circumstances.

"Nothing," I say quickly. "It's just disheartening listening to how fast these tales grow." I tighten my fingers around my satchel straps. Every hissed accusation, every furtive glance could spiral into something much darker before nightfall.

We leave the apothecary, stepping back into the crisp air. Hezekiah talks excitedly about a new shipment of cinnamon arriving, but I have trouble focusing on his words.

Finally, we reach the fork where our paths diverge. My home lies to the east, his to the west. I stop, my hands stuffed into my coat pockets, and glance at him.

"You heading straight home?" I ask, my voice sounding louder than I mean it to in the wind.

Hezekiah nods, his expression serious. "Aye. Make it home safely, Alexander."

I nod back. "You too, Hez. Be careful."

By the time I reach my small home on the outskirts of Salem, my fingers are numb and my cheeks sting. I step inside, shutting the wind and the clamor of the world behind me.

The house is cold, but its walls offer a small comfort. I set my satchel down, thinking of the cousins, Betty and Abigail, who are much younger than Phineas. I consider the way their shrieks have set half the town on edge. I was raised Puritan, yet I don't believe their cries are of the devil. No, it is mischief, boredom, the desire to see how far they can bend the grown folk, and I can't help but wonder how many will be caught in the trap of their own credulity.

Here, in the quiet of my home, I let myself see the truth beneath the panic: superstition can be power, wielded by the smallest hands, and even the most guarded minds may be fooled by folly.

WE SHALL CARE FOR HER

LILA

THE INDIGENOUS WOMEN melt back into the trees behind us, and a hollow shiver runs through me. For a moment, I had felt some measure of safety in their quiet kindness, but now I'm in Salem, a place where people are hanged, and the weight of history presses down on me, making my heart race as I realize how truly out of place, and out of time, I am.

Rebecca Nurse leans closer to me, her voice low. "Are you hurt? You must be frozen solid."

"Maiden," one of the women says, taking my wet dress from my hands. "What is your name?"

"Lila," is all I can muster.

A calm voice replies, "I'm Sarah." She glances at the others behind her. "This is Mary, Susannah, and Rebecca. We'll take you to Rebecca's house. It's not far from here."

Rebecca Nurse walks at the center, her back crooked and her shoulders slumped from years of labor and age. She moves slowly, her steps careful, as if each one takes effort. Her hands clutch her shawl, and her face is lined and pale, the skin thin from time and toil. She is meek and exhausted, the kind of woman who could never wield power over anyone or anything.

A sharp gust cuts through our line, and I shiver violently, staggering. One of the women grabs my elbow, her calloused hands steadying me. I let her, leaning into the support, feeling my legs tremble under me. My stomach churns, my throat is dry, and my pulse races as if I've been running for hours.

"Here," Rebecca says, pointing to a brick house just off the path. The others nod, easing me toward it with careful hands. I follow as if in a dream, half-suspended between the chill outside and the dizzying heat of my body. My head lolls against the shoulder of the woman beside me, and I feel weaker than I ever have before.

We reach the door, and the group gently ushers me inside. The warmth hits me like a wave, the scent of wood smoke and dried herbs filling my senses. My legs finally give way entirely, and I collapse onto the floor. Hands lift me effortlessly, carrying me to a small, feather-stuffed bed tucked into a back bedroom. Rebecca Nurse hovers at the bedside, pulling the blanket around me with practiced ease.

"You'll rest here," she says, her voice calm. "You're safe, child."

I close my eyes, a hum of voices around me, and the heat of the fire warming the room. Relief and exhaustion wrestle for dominance, but I still feel weak.

A small tray is set at my side, where a cup of broth steams, thick with the scent of carrots and onions, along with a small cup of water, clear and cold. I gulp the water first. Then setting the cup down, I grasp the bowl of broth, my hands shaking. The steaming liquid is soothing against my tongue, but my stomach still coils with unease.

"You must drink," Rebecca Nurse says, kneeling beside me. Her gray hair is tucked neatly beneath her bonnet. Her voice carries no impatience, only quiet insistence. "You look pale, child."

I nod mutely, sipping the broth as Rebecca's household stirs around me. A young girl, perhaps five, flits across the room, her eyes filled with curiosity. "Grandmother," she says, "who is she?"

Rebecca glances down at me. "She is a maiden named Lila, and she is unwell, my dear," she says gently. "No need for questions now. We shall care for her."

Another deeper, rougher voice, maybe a son-in-law or an older grandson, grumbles about the bitter cold and of how I nearly caught my death.

Their movements are careful, almost reverent, as if approaching a fragile creature. I study them quickly, realizing that this is Rebecca Nurse's family: a daughter, tall and sturdy, with a wary glance; a granddaughter, small and precocious, and a man with suspicion etched into his expression.

I close my eyes, trying to calm the panic rising like wildfire in my chest. Each detail I take in–the sturdy beams overhead, the woolen skirts and aprons–is proof that I am in the past. But my mind rebels against it. I have no name here, no explanation. If I open my mouth to ask, they will think me mad, and perhaps they'd be right.

Rebecca straightens the blanket around me one last time. "I'll check on you soon," she says.

The younger woman murmurs, "We'll leave you to yourself now. You need quiet."

"Thank you," I croak, my throat dry.

The click of the latch echoes in the small room as they leave, and I sink into the pillows, the hush around me pressing in. My eyelids grow heavy, and despite the fever, I finally drift into sleep.

FEVER BLOOMS LIKE FIRE BENEATH MY SKIN, MAKING EACH BREATH FEEL heavy, each blink a labor. My stomach aches, and my head spins with a fog that seems to thicken with every second. Rebecca kneels beside me, her hands firm on my forehead. "The child is burning up," she mutters, her voice low, almost to herself. "We must fetch help."

A voice answers quickly. "I'll fetch the healer." The footsteps fade, leaving only my ragged breathing.

Time stretches, and the room spins. Every sound, every shadow is dull against the fog of fever.

Finally, I hear the clatter of shoes on the wooden boards and a knock at the door. Rebecca rises and opens it to a poised woman who carries herself with a quiet authority. Her dark curls are lined with streaks of gray, billowing loosely, and her eyes are deep green.

"Good day, Mistress Nurse," she says to Rebecca, her voice calm and smooth. "I hear there is illness here. I am told the girl is feverish and weak."

Rebecca nods, gesturing toward the bed. "Indeed. She is ailing, and I fear the sickness will take hold. Please, see what you can do."

I squint at the small satchel the woman begins removing leaves from. "Is that feverfew?" I croak, pointing to a sprig. "And lavender… and… that looks like elderflower?"

The woman's eyes fill with curiosity. "You know these leaves?" she asks, her voice inquisitive. She kneels beside me, carefully spreading the herbs in front of me. "Most girls your age wouldn't have the sense to recognize even one of them."

"I… my mother taught me," I whisper. "And I've gathered and dried them myself. I know which to brew for fevers, which for pain, which to ward off sickness."

"Well, then you'll make this easier for both of us. Let's see how we can help you recover."

I nod weakly, trying to focus. "I… yes," I croak. "I have prepared teas of catnip and chamomile. The raspberry leaves are also helpful for fever."

She smiles faintly, a small, secretive curve of her lips. "You are wise beyond your years. We shall combine what we have. A tea of mint and elderflower, a poultice of yarrow and plantain, and if the fever rises, a compress of comfrey on the temples."

I watch her work, fascinated despite the haze of illness. She moves with deliberation, crushing herbs with the pestle, boiling water over the hearth.

I sip the bitter tea she hands me, and it seems to ease some of the ache. "Thank you," I murmur, my voice still rough. "I… I don't even know your name."

She tilts her head slightly. "Miriam Carter," she says softly. "I'm the village healer. You, my dear, have strength, even in this sickness. That strength will see you through."

Miriam settles into a chair beside my bed, her emerald eyes fixed on me with curiosity. "Child, tell me," she says, her voice calm. "Who brought you here? Who guided you to this place?"

I falter, realizing this woman won't know the word *indigenous*. "Some very kind women brought me here," I manage, voice trembling. "They're not English, not from this village."

Miriam studies me, her expression patient. "Ah," she says finally, nodding. "You mean the people of the land, the ones who know the forests, the rivers, the winds before us." She leans forward slightly, her voice dropping to a conspiratorial whisper. "The Naumkeag, the children of this soil long before Salem was here."

The women who helped me were Naumkeag, just as I thought.

"Yes," she continues, tilting her head. "They saw you lost, drifting between worlds. You are fortunate to have crossed paths with them. Few are so guided."

Her words hit me like a strike I can't see coming. How could she know this? Nothing I have said gives her any reason to, and yet she seems to understand. My chest tightens in panic, but I force myself to remain still, unable to voice the questions swirling in my mind.

"Some things happen outside the bounds of understanding," Miriam says quietly. "Not everything must be explained."

The soft shuffle of footsteps fades, the click of the latch marking their departure. I feel the heat of the blankets, and the quiet settling around me. My thoughts drift, scattered deep in the fever haze, and I hope, desperately, that when I open my eyes, I'll be back in 2025, back in my own time, back where none of this could possibly be real.

And then, finally, sleep takes me.

TELL US, TITUBA

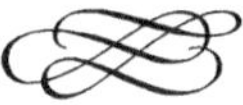

ALEXANDER

THE MEETINGHOUSE IS STIFLING. The air presses heavily, thickened by unease and sweat despite the winter outside. My boots creak on the floorboards as we follow my father down the aisle. He walks with his shoulders square and his chin high, as though he alone might steady the madness if it comes to that. My mother clutches her cloak at her throat, her lips pressed into a tight line, mostly due to fear of the urge to speak. She's afraid she may try to slip some sense into a neighbor's ear before the hour grows even more dangerous.

Beside me, Phineas bumps my shoulder, and his eyes alight with the restless gleam of curiosity. He wants to see it all, to miss nothing of the spectacle. On my other side, Hezekiah claims he came for the drama, but his fidgeting and apparent discomfort tell me he may already wish himself elsewhere.

Every bench is filled. Children squirm against their mothers, old men crane forward to hear, and young women lean in, eager for every detail. The talk in Salem has been fevered these past weeks, but now, with Tituba herself to be examined, the town gathers like bees to honey.

The accused sits near the front–Tituba. My father says she *belongs* to Reverend Parris, though I refuse to accept that "belong" is the right word for a human being. She is small, her skin darker than anyone else's in the room, and her deep brown eyes dart as quickly as a bird's from face to face. Her hands are folded in her lap, her wrists bound loosely as if to remind us all she is not free.

"She bewitched them," a woman hisses behind me. "Made the girls writhe and bark like dogs. I saw it with my own eyes."

I don't turn, though I wonder who would be ignorant enough to say such a thing. Though, I had seen some of it too–the fits, the shrieks, the strange convulsions. They were clearly not born of bewitchment and had nothing to do with Tituba. The strange actions are simply the fancy of two young girls.

The magistrates enter, and the crowd falls to a hush. John Hathorne steps forward, stern as a carved idol, and Jonathan Corwin is not far behind. They sit high so that all may see their faces, and I find myself shifting on the bench, restless.

Hathorne speaks first, his voice sharp as a blade. "Tituba, what evil spirit have you familiarity with?"

The room holds its breath. Tituba looks down at her bound hands, then lifts her chin. "None," she says, her voice soft, almost pleading.

Hathorne leans forward. "Why do you hurt these children?"

"I do not hurt them," she answers quickly, shaking her head. "They do lie."

But already the girls at the front, the afflicted, are crying out. Abigail Williams clutches her throat and gasps as though strangled. Betty Parris falls to her knees, shrieking, "She is upon me, she pricks me with a stick!"

The room erupts. Mothers clutch children to their skirts, men mutter, and Phineas grabs my arm in excitement. "Do you see? She does it even now!"

"Oh, Phin, you can't possibly be serious," I hiss.

Just then, an uproar rattles the walls. Hathorne slams his hand down upon the table, demanding silence, and the voices dwindle. Abigail whimpers in the front row, twisting her hands as though they are scorched. My stomach knots.

"Tituba," Hathorne thunders again. "Tell us true. Who hurts these children?"

Her eyes move about the room, settling for an instant on Reverend Parris, who sits stiff-backed and grim. Her master. Her jailer. Her voice trembles. "The Devil come to me," she whispers. "He bid me serve him."

A gasp ripples through the meetinghouse. Hezekiah stiffens beside me, muttering low, "God preserve us."

Hathorne leans forward, sensing his quarry. "The Devil, you say. And who with him? Name them!"

Tituba wrings her hands, rocking on the bench. For a moment, I think she will refuse, and some part of me hopes she will. But then her shoulders slump as though beaten down. "There be... two women, Sarah Good and Sarah Osburn. They ride upon poles in the night. I see them."

The crowd gasps again, this time louder, some voices rising in outrage, others in satisfaction, as though they have long suspected such names. I know Sarah Good. She is a gaunt woman who could scarcely harm a fly, and Osburn is crippled, barely able to rise from her bed. How could such women ride poles through the air?

Yet, the people murmur eagerly, taking Tituba's words as gospel.

Corwin presses next, his voice quieter, almost coaxing. "Did you see them hurt the children?"

Tituba nods, tears brimming in her eyes. "Aye. They pinch, they prick. The Devil showed me a book—great and black. I see many marks within–the names of Salem folk. And the women, they press the children to sign their names in the book."

A moan sweeps across the benches, and I see Phineas's face light with mischievous rapture, as though he hears a sermon proving all his fears true. I feel only a deep unease, my chest tight.

Hezekiah leans close, murmuring, "She tells them what they wish to hear. Do they not see it? Parris has threatened her and told her what to say."

I do. I see the way Hathorne nods, pleased, and how Corwin presses her, urging more from her like a man drawing water from a spring. I see how the crowd drinks in every word, their hunger growing.

"Who else consorts with the Devil?" Hathorne demands. "Tell us all, Tituba!"

Tituba twists her bound hands, her voice louder now. "Sarah Good sent her creatures upon the children. She set her cat upon Elizabeth Hubbard, clawed her, bit her. I saw the marks upon the girl's flesh."

Tituba's words come faster now, spilling in a rush. "And birds, black and yellow, I see them about her. They circle her head. They peck and claw the girls. She bid them torment, and they obey."

The afflicted stir at once. Ann Putnam lurches forward, clutching her arm as if scratched anew, and young Elizabeth Hubbard cries out, pulling up her sleeve to show faint red marks across her skin.

"She has a yellow bird in her hand even now!" Tituba cries, pointing with a trembling finger.

A shriek goes up from the front rows. "I see it!" Abigail Williams wails, her eyes fixed on some spot just above the magistrates' table. Elizabeth Hubbard nods furiously through her tears, crying that the bird pecks her.

The meetinghouse erupts in pandemonium. Mothers draw their children even closer. Men crane upward toward the rafters, some swearing they, too, can see the flutter of wings. My brother clutches my arm so tightly it hurts.

"D'you hear? D'you see? The Devil's mark upon her!" he breathes.

I look at my brother with disdain. "There's nothing there but shadows, cobwebs, and tall tales. The poor wretch speaks what they drive her to say."

Now Tituba weeps, rocking as though a child herself. Some women in the room begin to cry, too. Others nod fiercely, whispering prayers, clutching their babies close.

I feel dizzy, as though the very boards beneath me sway. I'm at a performance born of terror. The accused woman's shoulders shake, and I can't tell if it's more from horror or despair.

Hathorne seizes upon it. "And you did see Sarah Good and Sarah Osburn with these creatures?"

Tituba nods vigorously, her eyes wide. "Aye, they torment the children. They whisper in my ear when I pray. I see their shapes in the trees."

Gasps crack across the room like sparks. Some cry out, "Lord, have mercy!" Others mutter curses under their breath, already damning the accused women.

Beside me, Hezekiah grips the bench so tightly his knuckles turn white. "This is madness," he mutters. "The poor woman speaks whatever will save her hide."

Yet Phineas leans forward eagerly, his eyes alight. "Madness? Nay, it is revelation. God Himself unveils the Devil's tricks before us!"

"Phineas Paine, I am warning you one more time. You do not want to say things that aren't true, especially in regard to black magic," I warn my kid brother.

Corwin's voice is smoother than Hathorne's, coaxing. "Tell us, Tituba, how long have you served the Devil? Speak plain."

She covers her face with her hands, weeping. "I try not! I pray, I do! But he press me, threaten me. He say he will choke me, kill me, if I tell. But I tell now, I tell all!"

Hysteria spreads. One girl begins to convulse, and another cries out that she feels like she's being pinched. A third coughs so hard she falls from her stool.

Hathorne pounds his gavel on the table until the noise subsides somewhat. "Silence! We will have order!" He glares at Tituba. "You have confessed to compacting with the Devil. You have named Sarah Good and Sarah Osburn as his servants. Who else? You must tell us!"

Tituba lifts her face, streaked with tears. Her voice is faint but clear enough to carry. "There be many I do not know… strange faces, townsfolk, too. I see their marks in the Devil's book. I fear them. I fear they will kill me."

At this, a shudder passes through the room. I see men and women glancing sidelong at one another, suspicion etched deep into their faces. The infection of doubt has only just begun.

The questioning drags on until Tituba can give no more. Her words dissolve into sobs, her voice hoarse, her body trembling as if she has been wrung dry.

Hathorne leans back, his voice cutting sharply through the tension. "This examination is concluded. Tituba shall be held until further inquiry." His gavel strikes once, sharp and final.

Corwin's quill scratches the last word into the record, and the magistrates rise, their duty for the day finished. Guards move forward to take Tituba by the arms. She doesn't resist, only bows her head as if the weight of her own words has hollowed her out.

I watch her shuffle away, and a bitter taste rises in my mouth. She spoke what they wanted to hear, and they rewarded her with chains instead of mercy.

The girls shriek and point, spinning tales of birds and cats, and the grown men of this town, men I was raised to honor, swallow their stories whole. I can't fathom how the sight of a trembling servant and a gaggle of imaginative children has bewitched the minds of an entire village.

It's a performance, plain as day, yet they drink it in as gospel, turning idle gossip into holy truth.

A WOMAN IS NEVER SAFE

LILA

I WAKE to sunlight stretching across the small room, faint through the little window. A plate waits on the table beside the bed with a few slices of dried venison, a coarse roll, and a bowl of cinnamon applesauce.

My stomach growls so loud it startles me. I don't bother with manners and scarf it down. It tastes like the best meal of my life.

When the plate is empty, reality presses in again. I slump against the thin pillow, staring at the bare wall, and all of yesterday's questions come rushing back.

How did this happen? How did I slip into 1692?

The last thing I remember is walking across the parking lot. Then my foot slipped, my head hit the cold, hard ground, and everything went black. Now I'm inside Rebecca Nurse's house, just months before they drag her away to execute her.

The thought makes my stomach flip. Rebecca Nurse has been nothing but kind, and she is an elderly grandmother. How could anyone accuse her of anything but love and patience?

For now, I should be concerned about my situation. People here expect answers. Rebecca will soon be asking where I've come from, where I'm traveling to, and who my family is.

What am I supposed to tell her, that I was a law student in 2025, grinding through a job I hated at a Boston law firm? That I slipped through time like falling through a trapdoor and landed in the middle of the witch trials I'd only studied in history books and pretended to act out on a stage? If I say that, they'll call me mad. Or worse, they'll call me a witch.

I draw the blanket tighter around my shoulders. I need a simple and believable story before Rebecca asks. I'm sure she will walk in here and ask soon, and if I don't have an answer, I'll already be in danger.

I'm mid-reverie when Rebecca enters, her arms already full with another blanket, a steaming cup of broth, and a look of concern across her time-worn face.

"You've gotten some color back in your cheeks," she says gently, laying the blanket across my lap. "Drink this. It will strengthen you."

I obey, my fingers curling around the wooden cup. The heat seeps into me, calming my shivers, but not the dread building low in my gut. Rebecca hovers, fussing and tucking the blanket closer, brushing my hair back like she has done for her own children. Then she sits on the edge of the bed.

"My dear," she begins, "it is time you told me. Who are you? Where have you come from? And where do you go?"

The questions hang in the air like a noose. I force myself to meet her eyes. "My name is Lila Bennet. I was traveling from Boston with my family," I say slowly, careful with each word. "I was bound for a nearby town. A position awaited me there, caring for children as a companion of sorts, to a family in need."

Rebecca nods slightly, encouraging me to go on.

"But…" I let my voice falter, weaving the lie with threads of truth. "On the road, our small party was set upon by—by bandits. They scattered us. I ran, but I think… I think I am the only one who lived." I shape the pause, the dramatic quiver in my voice, the slight catch in my throat, all practiced and deliberate, like stepping into a character on stage. Every tremor and hesitation is for Rebecca, not for me.

She squeezes my hand, firm yet comforting. Her eyes glisten with sympathetic tears.

"I wandered for hours," I continue, spinning it now, desperate to keep the thread tight. "I would have frozen had not a group of Naumkeag women found me. They were so kind. They gave me food, guided me through the woods, and brought me to this village. Without them, I would have perished."

Rebecca studies me, her eyes wide, her mouth parted slightly, a hand rising to clutch at her chest. My palms sweat beneath the blanket, but I keep still, keep breathing, letting the pause linger. I watch her, careful not to let my relief show too plainly, shaping my posture and tone to match the fear and grief I want her to believe.

"Good heavens, child," she whispers at last, her voice trembling. "To endure such loss... to wander alone in the snow... the Lord Himself must have guided you to our door. You are safe here, truly. We will see you cared for."

I offer a small, grateful smile, relieved that she bought my story, and loosen my chest, but only slightly. Guilt replaces dread, as I hate lying to such a genuinely good old woman.

The house soon settles into quiet rhythms. Rebecca and her family go about their day, as I try to regain my strength and calm my racing thoughts, letting the warmth lull me, until a sharp knock rattles the door.

When Rebecca reappears at the threshold of my borrowed room, she's carrying a small bundle of clean clothes. "I took the liberty of washing and drying your dress, Miss Lila," she says gently, holding it out to me. "If you'd like, you may change, and Goody Martin has come by to visit. Do you feel strong enough to join us for tea in the sitting room?"

I accept the dress with a grateful nod, brushing my fingers across the carefully laundered fabric. The scent of soap and winter sunlight still clings to it, a simple comfort I didn't realize I needed.

"I think I will join you, thank you. And thank you, Goody Nurse," I say, my voice firm despite the tremor of nerves underneath. "For the dress, for the food... for everything you've done for me. For sending for the healer yesterday. You saved my life."

Rebecca gives me a small, gentle smile. "You were very ill, child. The Lord watches over those in need. It was nothing."

"It was everything," I insist softly, looking her in the eye. "I don't know how I could have managed without you."

"You're welcome here as long as you need." Before stepping out of the room, Rebecca gives me a tight hug, the kind that feels like what I've always imagined a grandmother's hug would be like.

I rise carefully, slipping out of the garments the Naumkeag women lent me and folding them neatly. I think of Naya and the others, grateful for their kindness, and wonder if I'll ever see them again or be able to return their clothing.

Once in my clean dress, I gather myself and follow the voices into the sitting room. The fire has burned low, but a pot of tea steams gently on the table, the soothing aroma grounding. Susannah Martin is already seated, her expression serious, a cup in her hands as she regards me with a polite smile.

"Good morning," I greet her.

"Good morning, Mistress," she says with a smile.

Rebecca motions for me to take a seat in the empty chair.

"I attended the trial of Tituba yesterday," Susannah begins, her tone sharp with lingering worry. "The girls, Abigail and Betty, shrieked and pointed, and accused her of all manner of things. And the men, the magistrates, they gobbled it all up. Every twitch, every convulsion, they called evidence."

"Were people afraid of Tituba?" Rebecca asks.

"Of course they were," Susannah replies quickly. "These children put on quite the spectacle. At one point, they started screaming that there were birds and bats flying around the room, which of course there were none. I fear nothing of the Devil here in Salem. It's the men who frighten me; men with authority, armed with words and law, who will believe anything a spoiled child cries out. Men who can destroy a woman's life with a glance or a question, and justify it with a prayer."

She sips her tea, her eyes fixed on the fire. "Tituba was small, trembling, terrified, but the judges, the men of Salem, leaned in, pressed her, coaxed her to speak what would condemn herself and others. And she spoke, because what choice did she have? I don't think she wanted to cause anyone harm, but in this village, a woman is never safe if the men choose to believe the worst. They decide who is guilty, who is innocent, and none can sway them once the hysteria begins. All because Abigail and Betty have nothing to do with their time besides conjure up tall tales."

"It is a cruel place, this world we live in," Rebecca adds. "We obey, we tend our families and home, we speak in measured words, bite our tongues, act just exactly how the men folk want us to act with meek and mild tones and demeanors, and yet, even that may not protect us."

I listen to the women, and I feel a familiar urge to speak my mind as well. "I wish I could gather them all up, give little Abigail and Betty a sharp tug by the ear and demand they tell the truth. They're just bored children, stuck indoors all winter, knitting and fuming because they have no work or play outside like the boys. If I could, I'd have them out in the cold, shoveling snow, hauling wood, doing anything to wear off that restless energy rather than turning it into hysteria, lies and accusations against their servant woman. I mean, come on. Isn't it kind of obvious that they picked the person with a target on her back already?"

Rebecca stiffens for a moment, as though she's unsure of what to make of my speech. Eventually she speaks. "Your words are—astonishing. I had not thought to speak it so plainly."

Susannah shifts in her seat, her brow furrowing. Then she leans forward, nodding slowly. "Aye," she says, "'Tis the truth. The girls do nothing but stir trouble with idle hands. You speak what I have feared to say aloud. We walk on a narrow path, and the men line the edges of the cliff. One false step, one glance, and we are shoved."

The fire crackles between us, and for the first time since I arrived, I feel a small surge of hope. They understand, even if they can't voice it freely outside these walls. Maybe, if I'm stuck here, I can at least do something to help change the past.

Maybe I can even save Rebecca Nurse.

TIME WILL TELL

THE SMELL of roasted chicken and fresh bread hits me before I even sit down. Father's already carving the bird, and Mother fusses with the serving dishes. My younger brother Phineas acts like he's starving, already starting on his second slice of bread and butter.

"Alexander," Father says, his voice low but firm. "Have you thought more about the Booth maiden? She's well-mannered and God-fearing. She's exactly the sort of girl to make a good wife."

I shrug. "I'm not thinking about marriage yet, Father. My hands are full with the farm and keeping the animals fed. Courtship can wait."

Mother huffs. "Courtship can wait, aye, but life won't. A man can't let his work take every hour of the day. Securing a wife, someone to *care for you*, to help manage the household, is part of a man's duties."

Phineas leans forward with mischief in his eyes. "And don't even get Mother started on her dreams of grandchildren, always wondering when you will marry so she can rock a babe to sleep once again."

Mother opens her mouth to chime in but stops herself. Instead, she lays a hand on Phineas's shoulder. "Well, Phin, maybe you'll give me grandbabes first," she says with a wink.

Phineas wrinkles his nose, feigning disgust at the notion of marriage, children, and even maidens. "Not I, Mother. You couldn't *possess* me to talk to Elizabeth Booth."

We all have a good chuckle at Phin's play on words and uncanny ability to steer the conversation back toward the crisis in the village. Devils, demons, witches and the like, are all Phineas has wanted to speak of the last few days.

Father clears his throat. "What have you heard about the goings-on in the village today? The trial must've stirred up even greater filth."

I put down my fork, folding my hands over the table. "I haven't heard anything today. I've been trying to keep to myself. The entire town has gone mad."

Mother nods. "Fear makes them believe in the Devil's work, and sometimes, that fear is enough to convince even the wisest of men that evil walks among us."

Father's voice drops a notch. "That's just the problem, my dear. The men we have chosen to lead us are not so wise, are they? Out there chasing devils."

Phineas snorts. "Bah! Let them chase devils all they want. I can't wait to sit back and watch them scare themselves fully cracked in the head."

Mother pinches the bridge of her nose, exasperated. "Enough of this devil talk! I've had my fill of fear and nonsense for one evening."

Father leans back in his chair, his jaw tight. "We need better men in charge, men who can think, who won't take every scream and accusation as gospel."

I nod. "Aye, Father. I agree with you there."

The meal ends, and we all help clear the table and wash the dishes. I thank my parents for dinner, and before I step outside into the evening air, I tell Phineas to take care of our parents and start walking home.

As I step through the chilly evening, the mention of Elizabeth Booth, the maiden my parents insist would be a fine match, lingers in my mind. She's only eighteen, barely grown into the life that my parents already expect me to live. Pious, proper, well-respected, just the sort of woman they imagine for me, but I can't stop thinking how little I know of what it truly means to be married, to be tied to someone else's rhythm for the rest of my life. And furthermore, I have always dreamed of finding real desirable love rather than just a match that makes sense to society.

The path home winds past the fields, brown and brittle under the waning light. I pull my coat tighter against the wind, trying and failing to push aside my parents' words. I can picture Elizabeth in her Sunday best, her hair pulled back neatly, with her hands folded as she listens to sermons and village gossip alike. She's respectable, of course, but respectability doesn't make her heart match mine.

By the time I reach my house, the windows are dark, and the air inside smells faintly of dust and dried wood. I push open the door, the silence greeting me, and step inside, letting the chill settle on my shoulders. The hearth is cold, the room still, and for a moment, the emptiness presses in. A wife, a companion, someone to share this quiet with… perhaps that wouldn't be so unwelcome after all.

I hang my coat and kick off my boots, crossing the room to my chair and sinking into it. I think of Elizabeth again. My parents have painted her in broad strokes: a good woman, suitable, worthy of any man's attention. I suppose she is.

However, what could I truly tell her? That I'd rather work my land than live up to society's expectations? That I'm not ready to play the role they've imagined for me? Or that I want a woman who sparks desire and passion in me, someone I can trust enough to let my guard down, and perhaps even fall in real love?

I sit until I finally feel warm enough to lift myself from the chair and tend the hearth. The irony isn't lost on me that I was so frozen when I arrived that I couldn't even start a fire, and yet now, in this cold, unyielding village, I can't help but wonder if a wife might be the one thing to make the house feel lived-in, to make the chill slightly easier to bear. Even as I tell myself I don't want a wife, the thought keeps tugging at me, a strange pull between freedom and the comfort of having someone waiting at home.

I finally manage to build a modest fire, the flames licking at the cold air in the room, and the warmth beginning to seep into my fingers and toes. Just as I step back to admire my work, a commotion erupts in the barn, and a sharp, panicked bleat cuts through the evening quiet. My heart jumps.

When I make it to the barn, I see one of the goats struggling to give birth. She's bleeding, and a bleat for help bursts from her throat as she thrashes in pain.

"Oh, Clara," I say to the struggling animal. "I'll fetch you some help, ol' girl. We need Mistress Carter."

I can't manage this alone without Miriam. Lantern in hand, I race down the narrow path toward her house, the cold biting at my face, my boots crunching over the frost-hardened dirt.

I pound on her door, my heart hammering. She appears almost immediately, as though she's been expecting me. "Mr. Paine," she says, reading the urgency in my eyes. "Whatever is the matter?"

"It's Clara, my goat," I gasp. "She's having trouble having her kid. I think it's caught sideways."

Miriam follows, a lantern bobbing in her hand, her presence reassuring. "Let's see her," she says, and we move quickly.

Back in the barn, the smell of hay-soaked blood is pungent, but I barely notice. The doe's eyes are filled with panic, her legs braced, trembling. I try to calm her, whispering, but she's too frantic.

Miriam kneels beside her, her hands moving carefully over Clara's flanks. I sink to the straw, my heart hammering as the doe strains again, groaning. Beads of sweat dot Miriam's brow, and she mutters under her breath, coaxing, adjusting, repositioning Clara gently. The tension in my chest tightens with every contraction the doe endures.

"She's close," Miriam says quietly. "We must keep her calm while repositioning the kid."

I kneel beside the stall, murmuring soothing words, though my hands tremble. Clara pushes, shivering, exhausted.

"She's strong," Miriam murmurs. "But it's slow work. Steady now… steady."

I nod, stroking Clara's flanks lightly, trying to help without hurting.

My stomach twists with helplessness, and I realize my mind keeps drifting, away from the labor, away from the barn, to the village, the trials, my parents, the life they want for me. I shake the thoughts off, focusing on Clara's straining, on Miriam's calm but commanding presence.

Minutes, maybe half an hour, crawl past. Clara strains again, and Miriam encourages her. "Push, Clara, push. We're right here, Mama. Almost there."

Finally, after what feels like forever, I see the first sign, the tiny head, slick and trembling, emerging into the world. Miriam's hands guide it carefully, a sigh of relief escaping her lips as she cradles the newborn. "Good work," she murmurs, brushing a lock of hair behind her ear. "You were right to fetch me."

I sink onto the hay, my heart still racing, my chest loosening as the danger passes. Yet Miriam notices the other tightness I can't seem to shake. "Mr. Paine," she says gently. "This isn't just about the goat, is it? There's something else on your mind."

I let out a short laugh. "Oh, it's the village trouble. You know, these witch trials, the girls making scenes, the hysteria."

Miriam shakes her head, smiling. "You're trying to convince me it's just that? Come on. You're sensible. That sort of thing wouldn't bother you. You know those girls are just pretending and looking for attention."

I look down at my hands, resting in the straw. It's not the trials that rattle me. "You're right," I admit. "It's... it's my parents. They want me to marry Elizabeth Booth. I barely know her, and they insist it's the right match. But I don't feel anything for her, and maybe that's foolish. Maybe love isn't that important, but I can't stop thinking that it should be."

Miriam studies me, her bright green eyes softening. "Alexander Paine, you listen to me. No matter what anyone else says, you must never marry without desire in your heart. Respectable matches, convenient matches, they'll make a life tolerable, perhaps even comfortable. But comfort isn't love. You'll never be whole if you marry for anyone else's opinion. Follow your heart," she says. "Even in Salem, even now. And if Elizabeth Booth isn't the one you desire, let her be. There's no shame in waiting for the one you truly love."

I lean back, letting the warmth of the barn's lantern and Miriam's presence fill the space. The kid bleats softly, nestled beside its mother, and I feel a small spark of hope, that some things—life, love, choices—can still belong to me, even in these uncertain times in this chaotic little village.

Finally, when Clara settles and the new life is safe, I help Miriam gather her things. "Thank you for everything," I say earnestly.

She nods. "Just remember what I said. Don't let anyone else choose for you."

I walk Miriam to her gate. "Thank you again, Mistress Carter," I say.

She nods. "You're quite welcome. And don't worry. You will find the maiden you were meant to wed. Time will tell that for certain."

I smile and bid Miriam farewell, watching her make it safely inside her quaint home. As I walk back, her last words echo in my mind. *Time will tell....*

Alas, time will tell a great many things—for this is Salem Village, and we are under a spell.

MR. ALEX

LILA

I'VE BEEN at Rebecca Nurse's house for a few days now, and the small comforts of her kitchen, the warmth of her hearth, and the quiet kindness of her family are slowly starting to feel like a refuge. It's a strange situation, settling into someone else's life, even temporarily. The weight of my story, the questions I can't answer, and the secrets I have to keep stay on my mind, but here, I can almost forget.

And then there's Catherine, or Caitie, as everyone calls her; five years old, with wide, curious eyes and a voice that can turn even the simplest sentence into something endearing. She flits around the house, talking nonstop, tugging at my sleeve, insisting I look at this or taste that. Despite her small size, she carries herself with a confidence I've rarely seen in a child her age, and I smile at her insistence on guiding me through every little corner of Rebecca Nurse's world.

This morning, Caitie and I are given our first task together. Rebecca wants a fresh bundle of herbs from the market for morning teas, and she has entrusted me to deliver her request. Caitie jumps at the announcement, her curls bouncing. "I can go too! I can show you!" she insists, and I nod, smiling despite myself.

We step into the village common, the sunlight warm on our shoulders. I keep my story in mind as we move among the villagers, noting every glance and sideways stare, memorizing streets and landmarks. The market square bustles more than I expected, with wooden stalls, shouting merchants, and baskets overflowing with fruits, vegetables, and dried goods.

Caitie bounces ahead, pointing enthusiastically. "That's Mr. Parris! He gots a big hat today!" she whispers conspiratorially, tugging my sleeve. I nod, pretending to examine him closely while keeping my voice low. "And that's Widow Putnam," she adds, wrinkling her nose. "She gots scary teeth!" I chuckle softly, thankful for her lightheartedness, even as I note the sharp, assessing stares of the other townsfolk.

Her little hand grabs mine as we navigate past the market stalls. "That's Mistress Corey! She gots a big basket of yummies!" Caitie hurries on, dragging me along. I let her lead, aware that she knows everyone in town, and yet I remain vigilant. Every step, every look from a stranger is significant.

We finally reach the herb stall, and I scan the bunches of rosemary, thyme, and sage, inhaling the faint comfort of familiar scents. Caitie peers over my shoulder, wide-eyed. "That one! That one smells good!" she insists, pointing at a small bouquet of herbs. I lift it, agreeing silently, and hand over the coins Rebecca gave me.

With the bundle safely in my arms, I follow Caitie back through the village, noticing details I hadn't before. The crooked sign of the blacksmith's shop catches my eye, and for a moment I can almost picture the McDonald's restaurant that stands there in my time. The wind stirs the leaves in the town square, and I think of the paved plaza that will one day occupy this space, now full of dirt and scattered stones. The harbor, just visible beyond the rows of low houses, looks the same, though the ships are smaller, the piers rougher.

People pass by, curious eyes darting to me, and I sense their suspicion even before I meet it. Caitie bounces along beside me, pulling me past narrow alleys that will someday host shopping malls and asphalt-covered lots.

Caitie knows everyone here—friends, neighbors, shopkeepers—and she greets them cheerfully, but my mind drifts between this moment and the Salem I know. There are streets I can't quite recognize, buildings that aren't there, and yet, somehow, it feels connected. For all the strangeness of the past, for all the eyes on us, Salem is my anchor, reminding me that even centuries apart, life here has a rhythm I can follow.

As we make our way down the lane, my mind mostly on the horrors that will soon overwhelm this place, I catch sight of a man ahead. He's tall, broad-shouldered, with a face that is so handsome, I can't look away.

As we approach, I can't help but stare, and before I realize it, I'm stepping too close to a cart stacked high with firewood. When I try to jump backward, my foot catches on a loose cobblestone, and I stumble, my heart leaping, and the herbs nearly slipping from my grasp. A strong hand closes over my elbow, steadying me before I topple over entirely.

"Careful there." His low voice is calm but edged with amusement. I lift my gaze to his striking blue eyes. He's even more attractive than I'd noticed from afar.

Caitie beams up at him and skips forward a few steps. "Mr. Alex! I didn't know you were here!"

His face lights with a faint, easy grin. "Caitie! There you are. Out running errands for your grandmother again?"

"Aye! Herbs! Lila helps me!" Caitie says, jerking a thumb toward me with pride.

He crouches slightly to her height, ruffling her curls. "Well, don't leave until I get you a molasses cookie from Goody Hobb's shop."

Alexander straightens, his eyes meeting mine, extending his hand. "Hello," he says, calm and steady. "I'm Alexander Paine."

I return the gesture, feeling the weight of his confident posture. "I'm Lila Bennett."

"Caitie," Alexander says, looking toward my little companion. "Do you think Mistress Bennett would like a molasses cookie as well?"

"Oh! She'd love one, Mr. Alexander!"

I laugh at her enthusiasm. Alexander winks at me, and with a polite bow of his head, he offers his arm. "Shall I escort you down the lane, Mistress Bennet?"

Glancing up at him, I feel my cheeks flush as I place my hand lightly on his arm. We walk, with Caitie skipping ahead. She chatters at him nonstop, and he listens, nodding, offering short, gentle replies.

Alexander leads us toward the small bakery tucked just off the common. Inside, the scent of fresh bread and warm spices makes Caitie clap her hands with delight. He steps up to the counter, returning moments later with a small bundle.

"Here," he says, handing it to Caitie. "One molasses cookie for each of you. I hope you enjoy them."

Caitie hugs the bag to her chest, her eyes shining. "Thank you, Mr. Alexander!"

I smile, taking my cookie with a quiet nod. "Thank you," I say, keeping my voice steady despite the flutter in my chest.

Alexander straightens, bowing slightly. "It was truly a pleasure to see you again, Caitie, and very nice to meet you, Mistress Lila Bennet."

Caitie waves enthusiastically. "Bye, Mr. Alexander! Come see us soon!"

"It was nice to meet you as well, Mr. Paine. Goodbye."

The warmth of the brief encounter lingers as he tips his hat and heads back down the lane, leaving us to continue our errand in the soft winter sunlight.

We thread back through the streets toward Rebecca Nurse's house. Caitie's mother, Mary, a kind woman, steps into the yard, her expression brightening when she sees us. "There's my little Caitie!" she exclaims, gathering her daughter in a quick hug. "And Lila, thank you for helping. You've been so good with her."

Caitie's father follows shortly behind, his gait sturdy and sure, calling greetings as he approaches. "Ah, teas from the market?" he says. "Perfect timing."

I hand the herbs to him, and their warm expressions and easy conversation pull me further into this small world. Still, even in the comfort of Rebecca Nurse's home, my thoughts fly back to Alexander and those mesmerizing eyes.

Inside, the house is filled with activity. Caitie runs ahead to help her mother lay out ingredients for supper, and I move to assist where I can, fetching bowls, stirring broths, and chopping vegetables. I work methodically, but my mind dances between chopping onions and remembering the chiseled set of Alexander's jawline, his stunning blue eyes, and that charming impish smile.

By the time supper is prepared and the table set, the evening sun slipping low, I realize that I am simultaneously part of this world and apart from it. Caitie laughs as her father lifts her onto his shoulders, her joy spilling over the quiet moments of the day.

I watch, my heart full, aware that somewhere in the village, Alexander has gone on with his tasks, yet I continue thinking of him. I find myself increasingly curious about him, wondering what he does for a living, who his parents are, and whether he's caught up in all the madness of the witch trials. I wish I could ask someone, but it would look suspicious and even embarrassing to ask Rebecca Nurse or her daughter.

Perhaps I'll ask Caitie later, once we're alone, and maybe she'll tell me more about Mr. Alex.

I'VE SEEN THIS ONE

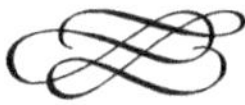

ALEXANDER

THE BITE of cold still clings to the air as I drive the axe into a length of oak, splitting it clean for the woodpile. My breath rises in clouds, the rhythm of chopping warming me against the lingering frost. Winter stores must last until spring planting, and every stick of firewood matters.

I have paused to wipe my brow with my sleeve when a sudden clamor drifts from the village common: shouts, shrieks, the sound of many voices tangled together. Then a sharp cry rings out, too shrill to be ordinary laughter, too wild to be neighborly chatter.

From beyond the hedgerow, down toward Salem, voices rise in a tangled chorus: girls shrieking, men shouting to hush them, women whispering behind their hands.

I set the axe aside as curiosity tugs me toward the noise. As I crest the small slope, I see a cluster of girls thrash and cry in the mud, their faces twisted and their hands clawing at unseen shapes in the air. I recognize them as Ann Putnam, Mercy Lewis, Abigail Williams; all three writhing and screaming as though seized by the Devil himself.

Everyone tries to keep back, watching, murmuring among themselves. No one dares step too near. At the center of the storm, the girls' hands shoot out, their fingers stabbing at poor Goodwife Bishop, who stands there pale, trembling, denying through tears that she has done them harm.

I draw in a breath. I know what this means—more accusations.

"Alexander."

The voice comes soft, at my side. I turn and find Elizabeth Booth.

She's not shrieking like the others, not crying out like Ann or Mercy. She stands still, composed, though her gaze moves between the girls and me.

"Elizabeth," I say, inclining my head. "I didn't expect to find you here."

"I was passing by," she replies quietly. Her hands are folded before her, neat and calm. "And then I heard the noise. One can't help but look."

I nod, my eyes drawn back to the spectacle. Ann falls to her knees, clutching her throat as though strangled by invisible hands. Abigail screams that Goody Bishop's specter is upon them. The crowd shifts uneasily.

"What do you make of it?" I ask, my voice lower now.

Elizabeth pauses. "I can't say for certain."

Her answer is careful, deliberate. I study her face, but she gives nothing away.

"Do you believe them, that Goody Bishop has bewitched them?" I press.

She glances up at me then. "It's not for me to judge. The ministers and magistrates will decide what is true."

"Yet you see them," I insist. "You see the girls contorting, choking, pointing. Do you not think it strange that it is always the same few who suffer so?"

Elizabeth folds her arms gently across her waist. "It may be strange, aye. Or perhaps it is the Devil's work."

My jaw tightens. "I have known Goody Bishop these many years. She sells cider at the market, works her own land, and keeps to herself. I have never seen aught in her that smacks of witchcraft."

"Others may see differently," Elizabeth murmurs.

A roar from the crowd cuts between us. The girls cry in unison, collapsing into one another, their shrieks piercing the air. Townsfolk gasp, whispering prayers, edging further from the accused woman, who protests her innocence with every breath.

Elizabeth's gaze remains fixed on the scene. "It spreads like fire," she says at last, her voice low. "One girl convulses, then the next, then the next. Whether it be truth or no, the people believe what they see." She draws a breath. "And belief can be as strong as truth."

Then, past her shoulder, I see Mistress Lila Bennett. She does not gape like the rest, nor lift her voice to the chorus of gasps. She watches with a level gaze, her lips pursed together as though holding back words she longs to say.

Almost before I've thought it through, I excuse myself from Elizabeth and step toward Mistress Bennett. My boots sink into the thawing earth, and the wind bites at my neck, but none of that matters. Curiosity pulls me forward.

"'Tis a scene, is it not?" I say as I come to stand beside her. "Half the village gathered, as though this were some traveling play."

Her lips twitch, almost a smile, though her eyes stay on the flailing girls. "A poor choice of a play, if you ask me. I've seen this one performed dozens of times already."

The answer startles a laugh out of me, quick and unguarded. "You don't think they're bewitched?"

She lifts one brow at me, finally turning to meet my gaze. Her eyes are a warm brown, yet they seem almost luminous in the pale late-winter light. I can't help but think about how beautiful she is. "Do you?"

I lean closer, lowering my voice. "In truth, no. I think they are children who suffer from idle hands and have found a way to command the whole town's attention."

Lila nods, her eyes back on the writhing girls. "It's winter and they're cooped up. They don't have enough chores to do, like the boys. They don't get to go outside like the boys. The boys all have work to keep them busy, but the girls just sit around, knitting all day, with nothing fun, no games, no toys, and, oh, my, no chocolate either."

I chuckle awkwardly, scratching the back of my neck. "Chocolate?" I ask, confused. "What is that?"

Lila lifts one brow. "It's… well, it's a sweet treat," she says lightly, as if the concept is obvious. "Something you eat to make life a little brighter. I just realized you don't have it here."

I study her a moment longer, the way she stands there, calm and clear-eyed even as the girls shriek around us. There's something about her that draws me in. I find myself wondering where she's from. The way she speaks, the things she notices–she is unlike anyone I've met in Salem.

Alas, it wouldn't be proper to ask. I can only let my curiosity gnaw quietly at me, hoping I might learn more in time, without overstepping bounds.

"You're *truly* not afraid?" I ask.

"Afraid of what, children with too much imagination?" She shakes her head. "No, I save my fear for real dangers. Hunger, sickness, men who are quick to point fingers when their own houses are not in order."

I study her profile, the firm set of her jaw, the way the wind teases strands of hair loose from her cap. She speaks plain sense, words I have thought myself yet scarcely dared utter aloud. To hear them from her lips feels like fresh air after a long winter.

"You are braver than most," I say.

"Or more foolish." She glances at me sidelong, as though to measure how I take it.

"I don't call it foolish to see what is plain before our eyes."

Her smile lingers, faint but sure. "Then perhaps you and I are of one mind, Mr. Paine."

The shrieks fade, little by little, replaced by murmurs and the scraping of boots as the townsfolk edge away. Even Ann Putnam and Abigail stop their writhing, though Mercy Lewis lingers on the ground, breathing hard before finally rising. The commotion that seemed endless now dwindles into scattered whispers.

"Looks like the spell is broken," I say, though my voice carries more amusement than judgment.

Lila lets out a small laugh, brushing a strand of hair from her face. "Or maybe the audience has tired of the performance," she says, her eyes following the departing crowd. "Either way, I'm glad it's over."

I glance at her, noting how calm she is, how completely unaffected by the chaos. "I've never met anyone like you," I say. "Most would have run from the noise, or joined in the accusations."

She shrugs, grinning. "I've got better things to do than conjure shadows."

I step closer, adjusting my coat against the lingering winter chill. "Better things, like what?" I ask.

She glances down the lane toward her quarters. "Like getting back home before my host thinks I've vanished into thin air."

I nod. "If it's not too bold, may I walk you?"

I believe I see a hint of mischief in her brown eyes. "I'd like that," she says.

We start down the narrow, rutted lane, my boots squelching in the mud. The village is quieter now, the bustle of spectators thinning, leaving only the occasional chatter from neighbors lingering near their doors.

"You're staying with Goody Nurse?" I ask after a pause, my curiosity pressing. "Are you family?"

Lila looks up at me, her expression neutral. "No, she took me in when my family was lost on the road to Boston."

I pause, realizing I've been prying. "Forgive me," I say. "I shouldn't ask so many questions."

Lila shrugs lightly, her eyes meeting mine. "It's all right."

We walk the short distance to Rebecca Nurse's house in companionable silence, the girls' cries now a distant memory and the village slowly settling back into its winter calm. At the gate, Lila pauses, glancing up at me. "Thank you for walking with me," she says softly.

I nod. "It was my pleasure, Mistress Bennett. Take care." She gives a smile, waves goodbye, and slips inside, the door closing gently behind her.

I like her more than I expected, more than I should admit aloud. With a final glance at the closed door, I turn and walk home, hoping that somehow, I'll see her again.

QUEEN OF HELL

LILA

REBECCA NURSE HAS BECOME MORE of a grandmother to me than anyone I've ever had in my life. I've been in her house for a couple of weeks now, and each day the warmth of her family wraps itself around me until I almost forget how strange and impossible my life has become.

Her daughter and son-in-law have welcomed me as if I belong here, and little Caitie's laughter is the kind of joy that makes the house feel alive even when shadows of the trials press in from the outside. Sometimes, when I sit near the hearth and Caitie curls up against me, I catch myself thinking this could almost be my home.

And that thought is always followed by, *Why am I here?* I can't push away the suspicion that it's because of Rebecca. History says she doesn't survive this year. Maybe I was sent here to change that, to protect her, though I have no idea how one woman with no standing in this community can stand against the tide of fear already swelling.

Alexander's face slips into my reverie, the way his smile dances in his eyes before it reaches his lips, the way his lips look so kissable, and the tantalizing realization that he has probably never even been kissed before. I blush just thinking about it.

Maybe part of why I'm here is Alexander, too. It doesn't make sense, but none of this does. And for some reason, I feel as though saving Rebecca and finding Alexander are threads in the same knot.

"Child." Rebecca's voice pulls me out of my daydream. She's wrapping up a honey cake with patient hands, the light from the window soft on her silver hair. "Would you be so good as to carry this parcel to Mistress Carter? It's fresh out of the oven, and I'd send my daughter, but she has her hands full with Caitie."

"Of course," I say quickly, rising from the bench. Anything to be useful.

Rebecca presses a small, warm parcel into my hands, wrapped neat and tight. "Miriam's cottage lies at the edge of the wood, eastward. Follow the path by the stream until the trees thin. You'll know it when you see it."

The walk gives me more time to think than I really want. I trail along the stream, the sun flashing on the water, and wonder how long I'll be here. Days? Weeks? The rest of my life? If I change Rebecca's fate, what happens to me? Do I vanish back to my own time, or stay trapped here in this one? That is, if I survive. What will I have to do to save Rebecca? Whatever it is, I'll be called a witch myself. If only I could remember what month Rebecca Nurse dies, and how long I have to prepare. I remember the names of the women who will die here this wretched year, but I can't remember any of their death dates.

The cottage comes into view just as Rebecca promised. Miriam's place is a lovely little log cabin with smoke billowing from the chimney and a crooked fence half-hidden by the bushes and brambles.

I knock gently on the door. A moment later it opens, and Miriam appears. Her dark hair with silver streaks is in loose curls, and her sleeves are rolled above her elbows. For the first time, I notice she isn't wearing a bonnet like the other women. Is she not a Puritan? Why would she live here if she isn't? But before I have time to consider it further, she steps aside, and I follow her in.

"Ah, Mistress Bennett. Lovely to see you," she says. "Come in, come in."

I step into Miriam's cottage. It's a simple, tidy home–the kind I'd expect in Salem Village, but shelves and tables are crowded with jars, bundles of dried herbs, and small bottles of remedies. The air smells faintly of sage and chamomile, and I realize quickly why everyone comes to her when they're sick.

I clutch the parcel until I remember to hold it out to her. She takes it, setting it carefully on the table, and unwraps the cloth to reveal a beautiful honey cake. She lifts it slightly, inhaling the sweet scent. "Thank you," she says. "Rebecca always makes honey cakes for me. They're delicious."

She motions me toward the hearth, and I lower myself onto a wooden stool, trying not to stare at her vivid green eyes that draw me into their haunting beauty.

"I'm glad," I reply, smiling. "I hope you like this one as much."

"It'll be wonderful," Miriam beams. "Would you like a slice?"

I hesitate for only a moment, and not just to be polite, but also curious, drawn to her unusual and captivating presence, I accept. "Please, and thank you."

She sets the cake on a wooden board and begins slicing it. Just then, there's a tapping at the door.

"Come in," Miriam calls.

The door creaks open, and a woman steps inside.

"Good morning, Mistress Carter," the newcomer says.

Miriam looks up and smiles. "Hello, Goody Carrier," she replies warmly.

The name hits me like a jolt. My pulse spikes, and a shiver runs down my spine. *Martha Carrier.* The woman I have studied for weeks in preparation for the play, the "Queen of Hell" herself, stands here in the flesh!

"Martha, this is Lila Bennett," Miriam says gently, her voice carrying reassurance. "Lila, meet Goody Carrier."

I manage a strangled sound somewhere between a greeting and a gasp. My hands tremble at my sides. *She's the character I was going to play. I know her lines, the stories they tell of her. And now she's here, and it's all too real.*

Martha lifts a brow, evaluating me. I swallow, nodding once, trying to steady my voice. "It's nice to meet you, Goody Carrier."

"It's nice to meet you as well, Mistress Bennett."

I nod, returning her smile, taking in every detail of her face and posture. She moves with a quiet confidence, the kind of presence that makes one pay attention.

Martha glances around the shelves crowded with herbs and jars. "Miriam," she says. "May I have some more of that iodine for my grandfather's goiter?"

I gasp involuntarily, and Miriam looks up at me, her brow lifting slightly at my sudden reaction.

Iodine. The word lands oddly in the room. I look at the small glass bottle Miriam reaches for on the counter, its simple label neat and precise, and feel goose pimples rise on the back of my neck and arms. *They didn't have iodine in the seventeenth century, did they?*

Miriam lifts the bottle, her movements calm and deliberate. "Of course," she says, handing the bottle to Martha, her green eyes moving back to me again, briefly, though she says nothing to me.

"Thank you, Miriam," Martha says, taking the bottle carefully. "I appreciate it. And it truly was lovely to meet you, Mistress Bennett."

"Likewise," I manage to say, my voice calm though my thoughts are tangled.

The door closes behind Martha, leaving only Miriam and me in the cozy cottage.

Miriam turns back to me, lifting the honey cake from the table. "Would you still like a slice?" she asks gently, holding the knife poised above it.

"I would, please," I say, grateful for the distraction from my racing thoughts. I sink onto the wooden stool again, trying not to fidget as she carefully cuts a slice and places it on a small plate.

We sit across from one another, and I take a bite, savoring the sweetness. Miriam watches me with a smile.

"The other night," she says, leaning back slightly, "I had to help Mr. Paine's goat, Clara, deliver a kid. It was stuck sideways, poor thing."

I look up, startled. "Do you mean Mr. Alexander Paine?" I ask, the name spilling from me before I can stop myself.

"Aye," Miriam replies smoothly. "That's the one. Clever and strong young man. Handsome, too. I was glad to help him and the little goat."

I feel a flutter in my chest. I've been wanting to know more about Alexander, and now Miriam is speaking about him casually, as if he's part of her everyday life.

"He has a nice home and his own farm. One of the most eligible bachelors in town. He's kind, hardworking, and well-regarded. I thought you might like to know, should you find yourself interested."

Caught off guard by the subtle suggestion, I swallow, my cheeks flushing. "Thank you," I say, feeling both flustered and delighted. "That's very thoughtful of you."

Miriam nods, cutting another slice of cake for herself. "It's always a pleasure to share good things," she says softly.

We finish our dessert in pleasant silence. The world outside seems distant, the troubles of Salem paused for just this little interlude.

Eventually, I rise, brushing my skirts smooth. "I should head back to Rebecca's," I say, gathering my thoughts and the plate.

"Do take care, Mistress Bennett," Miriam says warmly. "You're welcome here anytime."

I return her smile, feeling a curious mix of gratitude and intrigue. "I appreciate your hospitality, and everything else, Mistress Hawthorn."

Following the path back toward Rebecca Nurse's house, my thoughts drift easily from Alexander, intelligent, capable, and intriguing—to Miriam, whose knowledge and commanding presence continue to captivate me. Martha Carrier, too, lingers in my mind, our brief encounter leaving me to wonder how much longer she has on this earth.

I am filled with romantic longing, curiosity, and a quiet dread all at once.

BISHOP AND OSBORNE

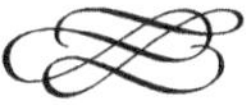

ALEXANDER

We get to the meetinghouse around mid-afternoon, at Hezekiah's insistence. He leans forward beside me, eager, his eyes scanning the men gathered in clusters around tables. He's here for the gossip, for the stories that move faster than any official word ever could.

"They'll be taken this eve," one man mutters to his companion, his voice low but sharp. "Constables will come calling soon enough."

"For those two?" another asks, shaking his head. "I thought this fuss over Tituba would settle everything. Let her go, and all would die down. Alas, it seems the town's aflame again."

Hezekiah elbows me, whispering with a grim look on his face. "Can you imagine? They're really going to haul someone off."

I shrug, keeping my voice light. "Tituba went free. Nothing came of her trials. Osborne and Bishop will be released as well. These men are merely babbling of things they know nothing of."

John Putnam is gossiping with Samuel Wardwell and John Alden, and we continue to eavesdrop. "Bishop has had her troubles before. Osborne, well… the girls have been pointing fingers, and the magistrates will listen. They must."

"Aye. Otherwise we risk dark spirits entering all of our homes," Alden agrees.

I chuckle, shaking my head. "The idle talk of this town is getting out of hand, Hez," I whisper. "These men stir up more trouble than necessary. Nothing will come of this witchcraft discussion."

"I hope you're right," Hezekiah sighs. "They sound like they know something we might not."

Wardwell's voice cuts across the room now. "They'll fetch Goody Osborne and Goody Bishop before dusk. Mark my words."

I glance at Hezekiah again. His unease shadows the intrigue his eyes once held. "Don't worry, Hez. It's all secondhand news."

"Not the first time I've heard the names spoken," Hez replies. "I have heard that Osborne's house will be searched, and Bishop, well, everyone knows she's far too outspoken."

The door of the meetinghouse swings open, and I lift my eyes. A group of women with baskets of quilting materials enters the room. Among them, Goody Nurse's daughter Mary, followed closely by Mistress Lila Bennett.

Seeing her, a rush of lightness hits me, and I can't help but grin. I have thought of her often enough, but never imagined she could stir me so, or that she could make my face betray me with such unbidden excitement.

Hezekiah notices instantly. "Looks like someone's taken by the sight of a maiden," he murmurs, elbowing me with a wink.

I scowl, trying to keep my composure. "Hold your tongue, Hezekiah Jenkins," I snap.

Lila glances around the room, and her gaze sweeps to me. For a fleeting moment, our eyes meet, and I swear she pauses, and I catch a glimmer of recognition pass over her face. She remembers me, and that's all I need at this moment to ignite the courage it takes to approach her.

I take a careful step forward. "Mistress Bennett," I say, my voice steadier than I feel. "It is good to see you."

Her cheeks color instantly, a soft, delicate flush that makes my chest ache with a curious warmth. She smiles a little uncertainly, and my mind scrambles for words beyond the obvious. She's lovelier than any woman I've ever laid eyes on.

"I'm glad to see you as well, Mr. Paine."

"Here to do some sewing?" I ask.

"I am, although I don't know how much help I'll be. I'm all thumbs."

I chuckle my response and offer a courteous farewell, though part of me longs to linger and speak with her for hours. However, I must not be rude and keep her from her work.

Reluctantly, I return to Hezekiah, who is smirking like the cat that caught the canary. "Come now," he jests. "Let us be gone before you set me to talking foolishness to the maidens."

As we leave the meetinghouse, I cast one last glance over my shoulder. Lila sits among the other women, arranging fabric with careful, graceful hands. The warmth in my chest doesn't fade, and I find my thoughts tangled between the memory of her beautiful face and the quiet, undeniable pull she has on me.

Hezekiah and I round the corner from the meetinghouse, and the street is alive with noise. We hear shouts, sobs, the harsh bark of men.

Then we see the commotion. Goody Osborne is being dragged from her doorway by Constable John Ballard. Her arms are flailing, her voice rising above the din. "You have no right!" she screams. "I have done nothing wrong!"

Behind her, Goody Bishop struggles, stiff and defiant in the arms of Constable John Willard. "Let me go, I tell you! I am no witch!" But the constables ignore the women, their grips ironclad.

Salem pours into the street, spilling from homes and leaning through windows.

"Take them! Lock them up!" someone screams.

"Get them away from our children!" another yells. "They're bewitched! They're of the devil!"

The crowd presses closer, shouting and pointing, their many voices clashing in a frenzy. Children cling to their mothers, some shrieking, others frozen with wide, terrified eyes.

The women who were quilting in the meetinghouse must've heard the shouting. A few of them emerge from around the corner, moving cautiously into the street. Lila follows behind them.

Before I can move toward her, Lila parts from the small group of women and starts straight toward me, despite the crowd and the chaos swirling around us.

"Mistress Bennett, please stay close," I implore her.

Hezekiah steps forward and looks at me expectantly. "This is hardly the time for introductions," I mutter, though I manage a quick gesture between them. "But Mistress Bennett, this is my dearest friend, Hezekiah Jenkins. Hezekiah, Mistress Lila Bennett."

She dips her head slightly. "It would be far better to meet under other circumstances. What is happening here is atrocious."

Hezekiah's mouth presses tight, his eyes scanning the crowd. "Aye. Never thought I'd see the day our neighbors turned on one another so quickly."

A man in the crowd shouts, "They're witches! Mark my words! Every one of them!"

Another yells, "Burn the devil out of Salem!"

Some women cry, "Witch! Witch!"

Their voices collide, a clamor of fear, anger, and disbelief.

Goody Osborne twists, kicking, straining against the constables. "My children! My children!" she wails, and a hush falls for a heartbeat before the crowd murmurs again, some whispering warnings, others screaming accusations.

Goody Bishop's face is pale. She glares at the people around her. "Do you see reason? Or only fear?"

The constables shove the women forward, forcing them down the lane toward the jail. The crowd follows at their heels, the noise rising and falling like waves crashing against the shore. Mothers clutch their children tighter, men shout over one another, and a few boys scurry after the constables, throwing stones at the ground near the women's feet.

"God deliver us," someone whispers behind me.

The air is thick with sweat, fear, and sour dread. Goody Osborne stumbles, nearly falling, and Ballard jerks her upright without a shred of pity. Goody Bishop does not falter. She walks stiff and proud, her chin high, but the look in her eyes jars me more than all the shouting.

At last, the constables push the women out of sight, swallowed by the mass of people trailing after them. Slowly, as if the tension has been bled out, the street clears. Doors shut, shutters bang closed, and voices fade. One by one, Salem retreats into uneasy silence, leaving only scattered whispers in the dusk.

I let out a deep breath. Beside me, Hezekiah rubs the back of his neck, his face pale. Lila still stands close.

"Are you well, Mistress Bennett?" I ask, my voice lower now, careful.

She nods, though she looks like she may be forcing composure. "As well as one can be after such wickedness. And I don't mean wicked witches—I mean wicked men."

Hezekiah frowns. "This town has gone mad. Today it is Osborne and Bishop. Who will be next?"

Lila's eyes brim with tears. "Who will be next, indeed. I wish I could remember."

"Remember?" Hezekiah asks before I get the chance.

"Did I say remember? I must've misspoken due to all the excitement. I just meant I wish I could protect whoever is next."

Her words strike me harder than I expect. Even here, surrounded by strangers, her first thought is for their safety, not her own.

I take a step nearer. "Would you permit us to escort you back to the meetinghouse? The streets are nearly empty now." I glance at the shadows stretching along the houses. "But I'd not have you walk alone today."

"I'd appreciate that very much. Thank you, Mr. Paine, Mr. Jenkins."

We walk with her in silence, the three of us moving through streets that just minutes ago were alive with screams. At the meetinghouse steps, she turns to us. "Thank you again. I hope I see you again soon." Her eyes linger on me for a heartbeat longer than courtesy requires.

I incline my head. "Aye. Soon," is all I can croak, quite stunned at her boldness. Most women would not speak such hopes aloud.

She nods once and disappears inside. The door closes softly behind her.

For a moment, Hezekiah and I stand in the street, then he exhales, shaking his head. "Alexander, I don't know what this town is becoming."

As we turn for home, Hezekiah still muttering about the madness of it all, I find my thoughts straying where they shouldn't. Goody Osborne and Goody Bishop were just hauled away in chains, their cries still ringing in my ears. Yet it's not their fate that weighs heaviest on me. Nay, all I can think about is Lila, and whether she'll be safe in this town, or whether I'll see her again.

And though shame prickles at the edges of my conscience, I can't deny my concern for Mistress Bennett eclipses the horror of all else.

HOW DO YOU KNOW?

LILA

THE MORNING FEELS HEAVIER than yesterday, as if the air itself is cut from all the fear running loose through the village. My stomach flips every time I picture the women's wrists bound, and the way the crowd pressed close, hungry to watch. I can't just sit still in the Nurse kitchen pretending the world hasn't cracked open.

"Goody Nurse," I say. "I'm going to visit Mistress Carter. Is there anything I can bring her for you or any message I can take?"

She glances up, worry already flooding her expression. "No, but do be careful, my child. The village is darker today, full of threats and accusations."

I nod, wrapping a borrowed shawl around my shoulders and stepping outside. The path to Miriam Carter's cottage lies just beyond the last huddle of houses, a strip of dirt threading into the trees. The further I walk, the lighter I feel, as though every step shakes loose the grip of Salem's watchful eyes.

When I reach her little house, I knock, and Miriam answers. She studies me for a beat, and I'm sure she knows why I've come.

"You've seen enough to worry now," she says, her voice serious but not unkind.

"Yes," I admit. "I'm worried about what's happening in town. It feels like a fever spreading."

"Then maybe the best cure is to slip away from it for a while. Tell me, Miss Bennett—" Her tone lilts, almost teasing. "Do you fancy getting tipsy?"

The question is so unexpected, I let out a startled laugh. "Tipsy? Here? That's quite impossible, is it not?"

"Not here." She tilts her head toward the woods. "The Naumkeag keep things the Puritans wouldn't dream of touching–fermented berries, roots that warm the blood, even a little smoke to ease the mind. Better than listening to ministers drone about devils."

I hesitate only a moment before answering. "Yes, I do want to get tipsy. Very much so, thank you."

"Good. Come then." She pulls her cloak tighter and leads the way, her steps sure as if she has walked this path a thousand times.

We follow the trail that Naya showed me once before, the memory returning of her soft voice telling me I could always find her if I needed to.

As the woods thicken, I steal a glance at Miriam. She moves easily, bonnet-free, her dark hair curly and loose against her shoulders. The question bursts out of me before I can smother it.

"Forgive me, Mistress Carter, but why don't you wear your bonnet? Doesn't the whole village champ at the bit to give you trouble over it?"

Miriam chuckles low in her throat. "I'm a spinster, child. I live on the edge of town and keep to myself… no husband to scold me, no father to watch over me. And when the village is fevered, or a babe won't breathe, they come running to me all the same, whether or not my hair is covered. They need me more than they need my obedience. So, they don't say a damn thing."

Her words ripple through me like a stone tossed in water, startling, defiant, and strangely comforting. For the first time in days, I feel like I have a real friend, someone who understands me and my attitude toward Salem's current state.

The camp spreads out in a loose circle, tipis patched with colorful fabrics swaying gently in the breeze. Small cooking fires send streams of smoke into the air. Baskets of berries, woven mats, and clay pottery sit in neat clusters, while children dash between the tents, their laughter ringing freely. It's a world apart from the rigid, fearful streets of Salem.

Miriam leans closer, her voice quiet. "These people… they've been attacked again and again. What you see here is all that's left of them. They are gentle, loving, and peaceful. If you stay a while, you'll see. They give more freely than anyone else you'll meet, and they've suffered more than most can imagine."

Miriam waves to one of the younger Naumkeag women. "This is Naya," she says, turning to me. The girl steps forward, curious and cautious, and I tell Miriam I know Naya already.

I smile at Naya, and she nods, her eyes bright, a small greeting that tells me she remembers me, too.

The Naumkeag exchange words with Miriam. Their tone is animated and questioning. Miriam responds fluently in their language, her voice teasing and coaxing.

Slowly, the expressions around the circle soften, curiosity and amusement spreading. After a moment, smiles bloom across their faces, and laughter ripples through the camp. Clay bottles of a strong, fruity drink are passed to Miriam and me, along with small platters of roasted game and berries. The smell of cooked food and the warmth of the fire spread through me. I take a tentative sip of the drink Miriam hands me. It burns sweetly at first, then settles into a strange, comfortable warmth.

Miriam throws her head back and laughs at something one of the older men says in their language. She's glowing in a way I've never seen in Salem, unburdened. She catches me watching her and smirks.

"Careful, Lila," she warns, her words slurring just slightly. "It sneaks up on you."

"I already feel it," I admit, and when I stand, the ground seems to quake. Naya steadies me with a quick hand to my elbow, giggling. I burst into laughter too, unable to stop, and the two of us nearly tumble into the grass.

It's strange how quickly I forget the dangers of Salem. Here, no one cares if I laugh too loud or trip over my own feet. Here, everyone is laughing with me.

Naya says something I can't understand, but the sparkle in her eyes makes me listen anyway. She hands me a cup, taps her cup against mine and motions for me to drink again.

"Don't you wish you could stay here?" Miriam asks suddenly, leaning against me. She switches languages halfway through the question, and the people around us roar with laughter at her joke.

"I do," I say, surprised at how much I mean it. "What did you say at the end?"

"I said, 'Don't you wish you could stay here, where people look at you strangely, not because they think you're a witch, but because you're paler than a mayapple blossom?'" Miriam winks.

I laugh far too loudly, and Naya watches me curiously, then reaches for my hand. She squeezes it once, firm and warm. I squeeze back, trying to tell her without words how grateful I am for her friendship.

The children run around playing jovially, and when a young man lunges dramatically, pretending to be a bear, all the kids squeal, scattering. Miriam shouts something in their tongue, clearly teasing him, and even I can't hold back my laughter.

My cheeks ache from smiling. Leaning over to Miriam, I ask, "How do you know their language?"

"Oh, Lila. Stick around and you'll find that I am quite knowledgeable about much."

I giggle, taking another drink of the warm, sweet blackberry cider. For the first time since arriving in 1692, I'm not scared, worried, or even thinking about the dangers waiting in Salem.

Here, in this circle of companionship, laughter, and generosity, I feel safe, and even loved. The Naumkeag people aren't drinking because it's expected or out of habit. They're sharing what they have to welcome us, to celebrate having guests, and their community feels alive, free, and human in a way Salem never could in this century.

Still, somewhere under the haze of drink, Alexander drifts

through my thoughts. He's the reason I don't *really* want to stay here, even though I like Naya and her people far more than I do the Puritan society I'll have to return to.

Eventually, Miriam nudges me, her eyes twinkling. "We best be off before the light fades entirely," she says, loud enough to carry over the laughter and chatter around us.

I nod, reluctantly agreeing. We wave and call our goodbyes to the Naumkeag, thanking them for their hospitality.

Naya lingers a moment, catching my sleeve. Her English is halting, careful, but the meaning is clear: *"If you need my help, I will be here."* My chest tightens, touched by the sincerity in her gaze. I hug her tightly, feeling the depth of an unusual friendship between us.

The path back to Salem winds through tall pines, and the evening air is cool on my flushed cheeks. Miriam walks beside me, her steps surprisingly agile for someone who's clearly had as much as I have. I stumble slightly on a root and catch my balance by grabbing the nearest tree trunk.

"Steady there, Mistress Bennett," Miriam teases. "You mustn't try to take the whole forest home with you."

I shove her lightly, half in jest, half in delight. "I'm fine," I insist, though the world is fuzzy in that soft, tipsy blur.

As we round the corner of the meetinghouse, the familiar streets of Salem Village stretch out before us, dim in the late afternoon. Up ahead, a girl steps out from the shadows, her posture rigid, a scowl on her face.

"Well, well," she hisses, her voice sharp enough to cut through the quiet night. "What have we here? Seems like Mistress Carter has been taking drink again."

Miriam snorts. "Seems you've discovered us, Mistress Booth," she says, her voice calm. "What a surprise. I had no idea that you were such a watchman."

The stranger's gaze shifts to me, sharp and accusing. "And you," she snaps. "Laughing, stumbling, swaying. Do you know what the town will say when they see you like this? Witchcraft, no doubt! I shall tell everyone what I've seen tonight."

I glare at the young woman, caught off guard, but the tipsy warmth in my chest makes me bold. "Witchcraft?" I repeat, incredulous. "This is the effect of blackberry cider. Or have you never been outside of the village? Have you never lived? Perhaps you should try some, and the stick in your bottom may fall out."

Miriam laughs so hard she nearly topples over. "Although, you know, Lila, this wouldn't be the first time Elizabeth Booth has called me a witch."

I laugh, loud enough that the sound echoes through the trees. "Aye. I've been accused of worse myself," I admit.

Elizabeth huffs, indignant, her fingers curling as if she might reach for something. "What could be worse than being accused of witchcraft?"

"Once I was accused of whistling while walking backward down the street," I retort.

Miriam cackles at my response, and for a moment, I think maybe we are all just in the middle of some overly theatrical rendition of a Salem witch trial play.

Elizabeth hisses at us once more, but then turns on her heel and storms back the direction she came.

Miriam chuckles. "Let us return to my house before Salem brings us more poked noses and wagging tongues."

We continue down the path, our laughter mingling with the whispering breeze. As we walk, Miriam begins humming a tune. It's whimsical, almost teasing, and it catches my attention.

I pause, frowning. That melody... I've heard it somewhere before. Tentatively, I start humming along, unsure why it feels so familiar.

Our humming weaves together like a drunken secret between us, and without thinking, the words slip from my lips. A song from 1967, yet, Miriam is humming it now—and I know the lyrics.

Miriam gasps, staring at me. "How do *you* know that song?"

WHY ME?

LILA

I HAVE no choice but to tell her the truth. My stomach knots, my mouth is dry, and the weight of Miriam's question hangs heavy in the air. If she knows that song, then she already carries the same secret I do, and it's one no one else in Salem could possibly know.

I take a deep breath and say it, letting the words out without hesitation. "I suppose there's no point in lying. I'm not from this time. I traveled here from… 2025. I was born in 2003."

Saying it aloud feels like stepping onto a scaffold, as though each word seals my fate in Salem. Even so, knowing Miriam must be facing the same impossible problem makes me feel I can trust her even more than I already do.

Miriam freezes, her eyes filled with wonder, as if the words have knocked the air from her lungs. "You… you mean, you've traveled through time, too?" she whispers.

"I didn't know if I could ever tell anyone," I admit, my voice shaking. "But knowing you've done the same thing… maybe I'm not completely alone after all."

She nods. "It was 1997 when I left my time. I was born in 1952."

I stare at her, my brain spinning as I try to do the math. "So you're telling me you are seventy-three? There's no way. You don't look a day over fifty."

"Yes." Her mouth twitches in something like amusement. "Time means very little once you know how to control it and once it's been torn apart."

We walk in silence for a few moments, as Miriam's cottage rises ahead. My thoughts spin faster than I can catch them. All this time, I'd thought I was alone.

"No wonder you know what iodine is," I blurt out as we step onto the little path to her door. "But… how did you make it?"

Her lips curve in a mischievous smile. "I was always a healer, and science was my passion before I ever touched a grimoire. In the 1980s and 90s, I ;earned how to synthesize iodine out of seaweed and a little magic. When I found myself here, I made it again, along with other medicines these people could never imagine."

She opens the door, and the warmth of her home swallows me, the herbs hanging from the rafters, jars lined up like soldiers on the shelves. The scent of dried sage and roasted coffee beans fills the air. Miriam busies herself at the hearth, starting a fire, boiling water, and finally pouring the dark liquid into two cups.

"You've been making modern medicine for them this whole time?" I ask as I take the cup from her, my hands grateful for the heat.

"Yes. They just think I know certain things because I'm a healer." She sits across from me at the small table. "They don't ask questions because they're so desperate for cures."

"I see. That explains why they all favor you so much and allow you to go without your bonnet. But if you don't mind my asking, you know Salem's fate," I press. "Why stay? Why not try to go back to your own time?"

Her expression softens, though her tone is certain. "I came to this era on purpose. I conjured a spell until I got it right. Mistress Bennett, this is where I am meant to be. I'm meant to help heal these people, with a little reasoning and a lot of enchanting. I am truly a witch, Lila. I don't hide it from myself, even if I must from them. I see what comes for Salem, and I accept it. If I burn, I burn. I belong to this place, and I always have."

Her sincerity rattles me. "Your ability to know yourself and your role in nature and the world is impressive, to say the least, Miriam. But… *why me?* Why did I end up here, in the middle of all this? These are terrifying times."

She studies me, her eyes catching the firelight. "Why do you think you are here, Mistress Bennett?"

"Perhaps to save someone… Rebecca Nurse, maybe, or others who will suffer."

I swallow hard. The names from history books echo in my ears. I never imagined being here with them, much less being asked to save them.

"Or perhaps," she adds gently, "you are here for Alexander."

The sound of his name makes my heart skip a beat. I lower my eyes to my coffee. "I don't know about that…"

"You will." Her voice holds that same sure tone, the way it was when she confessed her own secret. "Time does not take without giving. It has brought you here for a reason. The question is whether you will choose to embrace it."

I stare into the fire, torn between fear and hope.

A sharp knock suddenly rattles her wooden door. Miriam and I glance at each other, and my stomach turns over. Knocking always feels ominous in this place. Miriam rises and pulls the door open.

Mary, Rebecca Nurse's eldest daughter, stands on the stoop with her shawl clutched tight. Her face is pale and pinched, like she's been running.

"Lila," she says quickly, her eyes darting past Miriam to me. "I had to see that you were safe. They've come for Philip English and his wife. They're being taken away in chains."

I rise, the words hitting me like cold water.

"They've been accused of witchcraft," Mary says bitterly. "They'll drag them to the jail before the hour is out. I thought—" She looks around, lowering her voice. "I thought they might come for you too, Mistress Carter."

Miriam doesn't flinch, but I catch the faintest spark in her emerald eyes. "We are fine, Mary, but thank you for your concern." She takes her shawl down from the peg by the door and nods for me to follow.

The three of us hurry down the path. Torches burn in the distance as a crowd gathers at the end of the lane, their voices overlapping in a low, feverish hum.

When we reach the cluster, I see the scene unfold. Philip English is shackled at the wrists. His shoulders are straight, though his face is ashen. His wife walks beside him, the chains clinking, her chin lifted in defiance. Behind them, men with muskets prod them forward like they're criminals. A shudder passes through me. Salem is swallowing its own.

I don't notice Alexander until he steps close, his arm brushing mine. "Mistress Bennett, I implore you, please stay near me," he murmurs. His voice is calm, but his jaw is tight. He keeps his eyes locked on the prisoners as though he could will the constables to release them.

The press of bodies closes in around us. Whispers hiss from every side. I hear condemnations, prayers, judgments swirling together. Someone spits at the ground near Philip's boots. Another calls him a demon.

I edge closer to Alexander, and he shifts so he's slightly in front of me, shielding me from the worst of it.

And then Elizabeth Booth sidles past on my other side, her face lit by torchlight, twisted and eager. She doesn't look at me directly, but her lips widen into a sly smile as she leans close enough for only me to hear.

"You'd better watch your back," she whispers. "Or you might be next."

I want to snap back, to tell her she's wrong, that I don't belong in her world of fear and accusations, but I know better than to draw attention to myself tonight.

Ahead, the guards push the English family forward, and the crowd follows, a dark tide of judgment.

I glance at Miriam. She's keeping her composure, but her shoulders are tense. "This is only the beginning," she says under her breath.

Slowly, the crowd scatters, murmurs trailing behind like smoke after a bonfire. Some shake their heads, others whisper eagerly, but the chains are gone now, and with them, the spectacle.

Mary touches my arm before she leaves, her face pale. "I'll see you back at home, Lila," she says.

I nod.

"Don't be out late, Mistress Bennett. It isn't safe…."

"I'll be right behind you. I promise."

Beside me, Miriam exhales hard, folding her arms across her chest. "I've had enough excitement for one day," she mutters, her tone clipped, though her eyes are a darker shade of green than usual. She presses a hand to my shoulder, then turns and makes her way up the path toward her house.

In an instant, it's just me and Alexander. He tilts his head toward me. "May I walk you home?"

"Of course. Thank you, Mr. Paine."

We fall into step together, the crunch of our boots the only sound. I don't realize where he's leading me until we step off the road and into a narrow space between two barns, shadowed and private.

"Are you well?" he asks gently, his voice low.

I nod too quickly. "Yes, I will be. Thank you. It was quite the day, and the arrest…."

"Everything will work out. Please try not to worry."

I look down, then back up at him. "It's just that people like the English family will be fine. They have money and connections. They'll find a way out. But the poor old widows who have nothing and no one to help them…."

"Do you think they will keep them locked away forever?" Alexander asks, tears brimming his eyes.

"No, Mr. Paine. Unfortunately, I don't. I believe they will kill the women who aren't able to afford the means necessary to protect themselves."

"If you truly believe that," he says softly, "then you must be far more frightened than you let on, and yet... you are incredibly courageous and well spoken."

I feel a flush creep up my neck. "Thank you," I whisper, unsure what else to say.

His lips curl into a handsomely endearing smile. "And forgive me for being so forward, but you are quite beautiful, too, Mistress Bennett."

The words settle over me, warm and unexpected, and I feel a pull toward him I can no longer resist.

I step closer, and he wraps his arms around me. Warmth spreads through me as I rest my head against his chest. I've thought about doing this before, imagined it countless times, and now I lean up and kiss him.

He kisses me back with insatiable passion, and we surrender ourselves to the moment completely.

BLESS HER SOUL

ALEXANDER

THE MEMORY of Lila's lips against mine lingers in the back of my mind. I still feel the press of her body against me, the heat of her skin, the sharp intake of breath she made the moment our mouths met.

I should be ashamed. I know that. I shouldn't have kissed her, not here, not in the village, and certainly not when the smallest rumor could destroy reputations, ruin lives, or worse. And yet, I cannot deny that our kiss has burrowed into me, a fire that refuses to die down.

I pace in my small sitting room, my hands clasped behind my back. Every shadow in the room feels alive, a whispering witness to my indiscretion. The thought of someone having seen us makes my chest tighten. My father's voice, the neighbors' whispers, the church elders' judgmental stares–I can already hear them all. It *was* wrong, and I know it, but the adoration I feel for her draws me to her, wild and untamable. Lila has captured me entirely, and I fear that there is no return from this.

The knot in my stomach tightens. This town thrives on rumors, and a man of my standing can't afford even a hint of scandal. Yet, all I can think about is her, how sure she is when she speaks, how clever she is, and how she moves with that strange, graceful charisma that feels out of place among the women our age here. And every moment of my guilt is intertwined with a fierce longing I can't battle any longer. I know that if I see her again, I'll have even less self-control.

Before I can spiral further, a frantic pounding comes at the door, and Hezekiah's voice slices through. "Alexander! You must come. Now!"

My chest hammers. "What is it?"

He bursts inside with flushed cheeks and eyes filled with terror. "Bridget Bishop. They're going to hang her. Everyone's gathered already. You must come!"

My brother Phineas follows Hez closely, his expression grim. "Can we stop them, Alexander? Goody Bishop isn't really a witch!"

I exchange a quick glance with Hezekiah. His hand rests on my shoulder, heavy with urgency. I grab my coat and follow them into the night. Torchlight spills across the empty streets, shadows leaping against the crooked houses.

The closer we get to the town center, the heavier the crowd becomes. The murmur of voices rises into a low roar, punctuated by gasps, cries, and the occasional shout. Every step pulls me deeper into a horror that feels like a dream.

When I reach the center, Bridget Bishop is already in position. She stands on the scaffold, a figure of defiance and terror all at once. Her dress clings damply to her skin. Her hands are chained, and her face is pale but resolute. I feel my stomach twist violently, the bile rising as I see her shoulders straight despite the knowledge of what is coming.

I respect Goody Bishop, and how she boldly runs a tavern in a town where men pretend not to drink, how she dresses in bright colors in a town where women pretend to be meek. I respect her independence, and inability to pretend she's someone she isn't, even with a noose around her neck. She stands defiant, refusing to admit to being a witch because she's not. She's simply a woman who is not afraid to speak up, and that terrifies the men of this town.

The crowd presses in, a writhing sea of judgment and curiosity. The men with muskets flanking the scaffold look rigid, their expressions hollow, as though they are aware of the cruelty of their task but unmoved by it. The rope hangs like a noose of inevitability, coiled and waiting for the final act.

I clench my fists, my nails digging into my palms. I've called every single member of the crowd a friend, yet each seems complicit in this atrocity. I feel the weight of betrayal, not just to Bridget, but to justice, to decency, to humanity. How can a town of neighbors, friends, and churchgoers become executioners so easily?

Hezekiah steps beside me, his jaw tight, his eyes moving nervously toward the scaffold. "It's... it's worse than I imagined," he mutters, his voice low, almost swallowed by the murmurs of the crowd. "They started with saying that she poisoned her cat, made wicked dolls, and that they wouldn't let her share the Lord's supper come Sunday...."

Phineas's hands shake as he grips the edge of my sleeve. "They're... they're really going to hang her?" he asks, the words taut with disbelief. "And everyone is just going to watch? Isn't there something we can do, Alexander?"

I swallow hard, the bitter tang of fear and anger on my tongue. "If we speak up, they'll arrest us too," I manage to reply, though shame envelops every word.

The executioner moves with calculated efficiency, adjusting the noose. Bridget's eyes meet mine for a fraction of a second, and in that instant, I ask the Lord to bless her soul. The village has made up its mind, and there is no escape from this horror.

Then I see Lila standing on the edge of the crowd, her face pale and drawn, her eyes filled with sorrow as they lock with mine. Without thinking, I push through the crowd.

When I reach Lila's side, I place a hand lightly on her shoulder. "Are you well?" I ask.

She shakes her head slightly. "I will be," she whispers. "I just... I can't bear to watch."

I squeeze her shoulder. "You don't have to. I'll stay with you. Look at me."

The crowd falls silent as the executioner gives the final signal. The trapdoor is released. A sharp, terrifying snap cuts through the night air as Bridget Bishop plummets, the rope taut around her neck. Her body jerks violently, and the sickening sound of her neck snapping fills the air.

Gasps and cries erupt from the crowd. Some vomit. Some turn away. Some stare frozen in disbelief. I feel bile rise in my throat as though the rejection I feel toward the cruelty, the finality, and the absolute injustice, is rising up from within me.

I glance at the crowd, at faces I once recognized as neighbors and friends. Now, the betrayal stings sharply, slicing through me.

I murmur quietly, "It's over. She's gone."

Slowly, carefully, I guide Lila away from the scaffold, from the crowd, from the eyes of those who gossip and speculate. Each step feels heavy, the weight of what we have seen pressing on us both.

We reach the quieter streets, shadows from the torches dwindling behind us. The night feels colder now, filled with gloom. I can still hear the distant murmurs of the crowd, the echoes of injustice hanging in the air like smoke.

Finally, I lead her to the Nurse family's door. "You're safe," I whisper. "Try to get some rest, and I will send Mistress Carter with some tea to calm your nerves."

She looks up at me, still trembling, and nods. "Thank you, Mr. Paine. That may help some."

"Please, call me Alexander. Mr. Paine is far too formal for what we've experienced and endured together now, wouldn't you say?"

She nods and then crumples into my chest. I hold her close, never wanting to let go, wanting nothing more than to kiss her delicate, supple lips, yet knowing there could be eyes lurking in every corner of this fragile town, eyes that turn to tongues and pour out venomous gossip.

I wait for a heartbeat, unwilling to leave her, unwilling to let go. The savagery of what we have witnessed will not leave us tonight, but at least here, in this quiet corner, we are safe from the brutality of Salem—for now.

DANGEROUS ROMANCE

ALEXANDER

THE STREETS ARE QUIETER than I expect, the torches that once marked the execution fading into scattered glimmers behind me. The air still carries the acrid tang of death, fear, and grief, and I can't shake the memory of Bridget Bishop's body jerking against the rope. Each step toward Mistress Carter's house feels heavy, as though the weight of what we've seen is pressing down on my chest.

I knock on her door, and a moment later, Miriam appears, her face calm and composed as always. Her eyes catch mine, and I know she's read the sorrow and anger waning behind them.

"Mistress Carter," I begin, my voice low. "I wanted to tell you that Bridget Bishop was hanged tonight." I pause, seeing her expression shift, though it remains unreadable. "I thought perhaps you might have something that could help calm Lila's nerves? She's… shaken, as anyone would be."

Miriam tilts her head thoughtfully. "Aye. Such terror and injustice would unsteady anyone's spirit. I do have a few herbal teas and tinctures that bring ease to the mind."

"I thought you might," I say. My throat tightens at the thought. "I fear I can't do much, but I want her to feel some comfort."

Miriam's eyes soften. "She is remarkable," she replies. "And it seems you've noticed. Tell me, Alexander, do you intend to court her?" Her tone is light, teasing, but her gaze searches mine, wise and knowing.

I hesitate, feeling a heat rise to my cheeks. "Indeed, I do," I admit. "In fact, I think we might already be courting, in a way." My words hang in the air for only a heartbeat before I add, "We kissed."

Miriam lets out a small, exaggerated gasp, feigning scandal. "Oh!" she says, covering her mouth, though a faint smile tugs at the corners of her lips. "Well, that certainly clarifies things. Then why don't you help me bring the tea, hmm?"

I can't help but smile, a brief relief in the midst of all this grief. "Of course," I reply, bowing slightly.

We move together into her kitchen, Miriam gathering the ingredients.

As we make our way back toward Lila, Miriam's voice breaks my thoughts. "She will be safe with you here, Alexander. You'll protect her, but you must promise me one thing."

I look Mistress Carter directly in the eye. "Promise you?"

"Aye. You must promise me, when the time comes that the young Mistress Bennett tells you her deepest most personal secret, you will believe her and you will not be as judgmental as this tiny, pathetic town."

Uncertain of what Miriam's speaking of, I agree to the terms of the vow, knowing Lila could tell me anything, and I'd still want to be by her side. "Aye. I promise."

Miriam and I step into the night air. Each step toward the Nurse house feels heavier than the last, the memory of Bridget Bishop's hanging flashing before my eyes.

When we arrive, the door is already open, and the faint murmur of voices drifts out. I can see Rebecca Nurse sitting stiffly in the sitting room, her hands folded in her lap, her face drawn and pale. Beside her, her daughter Mary rocks little Caitie gently, whispering reassurances to the five-year-old who clings to her mother. Mary's husband sits nearby, his jaw tight, his eyes shadowed with grief. And there, on the other side of the room, Lila sits rigid, her hands folded in her lap, her gaze distant.

"Mr. Alexander," Caitie chirps as we enter, her small voice ringing out. "Are you here with Miss Miriam?" She tilts her head curiously then ducks behind her mother's skirts.

"Aye, Caitie," I reply softly, kneeling to her level for a moment. "We're here to check on you and your family. How are you, little one?"

"I'm sad, Mr. Alexander."

"I'm sad, too, Cait."

"Let's get the tea to them before anyone faints from shock," Miriam murmurs.

I follow her lead, setting the steaming cups carefully on the low table. The fragrance of chamomile settles over the room, a fragile comfort against the horror of the day.

We make the tea and all sit together, the quiet punctuated only by the soft clink of porcelain and the occasional sigh. I watch Lila as she takes a tentative sip of tea, her hands wrapped around the warm cup. She meets my eyes briefly, and I can see the tremor in her lips, the way her fingers shake slightly. My chest tightens.

"This could happen to anyone," Rebecca says gravely, her voice low, carrying the power of her grief. "No one is safe when fear rules a town."

Mary's voice is filled with emotion. "And yet… we sit here, and they *will* hang another. How do we go on knowing that?" Her gaze drifts toward her husband as if seeking reassurance, or perhaps a shared disbelief.

Lila speaks up, her eyes glistening. "It doesn't matter what you're accused of when the wrong men are left in charge for too long."

"Aye. And, we must remember Goody Bishop for who she truly was," I add. "Not for the lies, not the whispers, but the woman who lived boldly, who refused to pretend she was meek."

Mary's husband, John, leans forward, his lips tight, his eyes dark with anger. "Aye, Mr. Paine," he says quietly. "You speak the truth. This town has lost its way, letting fear and superstition rule where reason should stand. Goody Bishop, any of the accused–it could have been any one of us. And yet they cheer for her death as if it were justice. I can't abide it."

"What is there to be done?" Mary asks.

"Aye… what is there to be done?" Goody Nurse repeats.

I rise, running my hand through my hair, anxiety pulling me to my feet. "Lila," I say as calmly as possible, "would you help me carry these empty cups back into the kitchen?"

She nods, and together we move quietly, balancing the cups on the tray. The kitchen smells faintly of teas and tinctures, the scents of Miriam's careful preparations. Lila's eyes meet mine, and in them, I see a trembling mix of sorrow and relief.

"I'm glad you're here," she says, her voice barely above a whisper. "With all that's happened, I don't know what I would have done if you hadn't come back to check on me. Thank you, Alexander."

I open the kitchen door silently, and we step onto the back porch, the evening air cool against our faces. The torches in the streets are long since extinguished, and the only sound is the faint creak of the house settling, the distant hoot of an owl. I glance at her, and without thinking, I take her hand, guiding her forward.

We lean against the railing together, close enough that our shoulders touch, and my fingers entwine with hers. The night is calm, a sharp contrast to the chaos of the evening.

"Alexander, it's dangerous for us to be romantic with one another, isn't it?" she asks, and her voice trembles slightly.

I bring my other hand up to her cheek, gently brushing back a stray lock of hair. "Aye," I murmur. "Alas, even with all that's happening in the village with the accusations, I can't stay away from you, Lila."

She smiles, her gorgeous amber eyes shimmering in the pale moonlight, and I feel the fire inside me ignite again.

I catch her face in my hands, letting my thumbs trace the planes of her flushed cheeks, tilting her toward me. Her eyes burn wild and comforting, like a new fire on the coldest winter night. Her ebony curls escape her bonnet, framing her face, teasing the fantasies I've dared to imagine, the ones where her hair tumbles free across her bare shoulders. Her soft lips, the shape and color of a cardinal flower petal, demand nothing less than all of my attention.

Witchcraft be damned. Villagers be damned. I kiss her with such intensity that all of heaven and earth together couldn't keep me from her lips.

DEADLY RUMORS

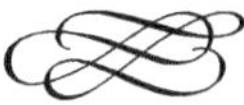

LILA

I WALK beside Caitie toward the market, her small hand tucked into mine. Caitie skips, humming a little tune, her basket bouncing against her side. I try to match her cheer, but there's a heaviness in my chest I can't shake.

We stop at a stall where a woman sells freshly gathered chestnuts, her apron smudged with soil. I smile politely, fumbling for coins, and two men's voices carry from just behind us.

"The English family's still in a Boston jail," one says. "They say they'll not return to Salem at all, lest the magistrates take hold of them again."

The other man spits into the dirt. "Best that way. Their name's tainted. Wouldn't want their trouble spreading here."

Their words send a shiver down my spine. I remember reading about Philip and Mary English. Their wealth and powerful friends bought them a kind of safety no one else had. They slipped free of Salem's grip and remade their lives in New York. It was smart, survival by any means, but the others... the ones without coin or influence, like Bridget Bishop, had no such escape. They were dragged to trial, condemned, and silenced forever.

"Lila?" Caitie tugs my sleeve. "Are we to buy the chestnuts or not?"

I force myself to nod, and to hand over the coins with a 'thank you' that sounds hollow in my ears.

We move deeper into the market, past the butcher's stall and the place where a girl sells candles, where a different conversation reaches me.

"Strange one, that girl," a woman murmurs just loud enough for me to catch. "Her manner of speaking. She's from no place I know. What did ye say her name was?"

"Aye," another voice replies. "Mistress Bennett. T'was Elizabeth Booth who first told me she witnessed her chanting a spell."

My heart slams into my ribs. My steps falter, and I bump into Caitie, who frowns up at me. Voices blur into the rush of blood in my ears.

Now they're talking about me.

Panic grips me by the throat, and I clutch Caitie's hand tighter, too tight, and she yelps in protest. "Lila! You're hurting me!"

I let go instantly, crouching to her level, my breath ragged. "I'm so sorry, Caitie. I'm sorry. I just—" My eyes dart to the corners of the square, searching faces for judgment, for suspicion. Every glance feels heavy, every passing look sharper than a knife.

I know what happens to women branded as witches. I've read all the firsthand accounts, seen all the movies and plays. But this is real life, and now it's my own name whispered in the same tone.

I squeeze Caitie's hand again, gentler this time, and force myself to remain calm. "We need to hurry home now."

The little girl peers up at me, puzzled but obedient, and together we step quickly from the market square, my pulse racing faster than my feet.

When Rebecca Nurse's house comes into view, relief loosens something in my chest. We step inside the kitchen where Rebecca kneads pie dough and I hand her the basket of chestnuts.

"Lila." She greets me warmly, but her gaze sharpens when she looks at my face. "What troubles you?"

I hesitate, then shake my head. "Thank you for asking, but I'll visit with you another time, Goody Nurse. For now, could you please tell me the way to Alexander Paine's home?"

Her brows rise, but she nods, giving me clear directions through the woods and over the ridge. I thank her quickly and set off, my skirts tangling in the brambles, my heart thrumming with every step.

The walk feels much longer than it actually is, but at last the trees open to a clearing where a modest house sits. Alexander steps out, shading his eyes against the sun.

"Lila?" His voice carries surprise, then concern when he sees my expression.

I quicken my pace until I'm standing before him, breathless. "I overheard people speaking about the English family. They're being held in Boston still, and folk say they won't return to Salem, for fear of more punishment."

He nods slowly, but his eyes search mine. "Aye. I certainly can't blame them for leaving town. I've considered it many times myself."

I wring my hands, anxiety and dread knotting together. "Alexander, I also heard whispers of my name. They said my way of speaking is strange, that I know information I shouldn't. They think I might be a witch, Alexander." The word tastes like ash in my mouth.

His brow furrows, but instead of recoiling, he steps closer. "Lila, listen to me. I know you are no witch. You are clever, curious, and braver than anyone I know, and people here—"

He gestures vaguely toward the village. "They fear what they don't understand. That is not your burden to bear."

I bite my lip, tears threatening. "But if the gossip grows, if someone speaks against me, you know what will happen."

He holds my gaze, his voice calm, unshakable. "I will always stand with you, and if the danger grows too great, we will leave. Just as the English family fled, we would leave Salem behind."

The thought startles me. Leave? Run--like fugitives? And yet, the idea carries a strange glimmer of hope, too.

I draw a trembling breath. "You'd do that? For me?"

"For you, I would do anything," he says plainly. "You're worth far more to me than this farm."

I have never known anyone to show me love or selflessness in this way. Back home, affection always felt fleeting, conditional, something that could be withdrawn as quickly as it was offered. With Alexander, it's different. He doesn't question. He doesn't falter. He stands on morals and values, and puts me before himself. In a world unraveling with suspicion and fear, his devotion feels like the rarest treasure. For the first time in my life, I feel truly seen, and the knowledge stirs something in me that is both frightening and beautiful.

"Thank you," I whisper.

Alexander reaches out and takes my hand. His palm is warm, roughened by work, but the touch is gentle.

I lift my eyes to his, and trust, fear, and the fragile thread of hope weaves between us. He leans in, just slightly, and I rise onto my toes.

Our lips meet in the faintest of kisses, soft but searing all at once. It lasts only a heartbeat, yet in that instant, the chaos of Salem, the trials, the whispers, the looming gallows, all fade into silence. All that remains is the press of his hand around mine and the quiet promise in his closeness.

When we part, I exhale shakily. He doesn't look away, but his thumb brushes the back of my hand once before he releases me.

"I will see you safely back," he says.

We walk together through the winding path toward Rebecca Nurse's house, the forest pressing close on either side, the crunch of leaves beneath our feet the only sound. My thoughts whirl as fast as my heart. I think of how wonderful it would be to stay with him in the safety of his home, but such a thing would never be seen as proper. A woman under a man's roof without kin or marriage would be enough to draw rumors, and here, rumors are deadly. They would call us wicked, accuse us of witchcraft, claim the Devil worked between us. The very thought makes my skin prickle, even as the longing to remain by his side tugs at me with a dangerous sweetness.

Finally, the trees thin, and Rebecca's house comes into view, its thatched roof silvered by the late sun. Relief washes through me at the sight, until I notice the cluster of figures gathered at the gate.

Men on horseback with stern faces. The glint of metal shackles in one man's hand.

My stomach lurches.

Oh, no! Not Rebecca!

"Stay close," Alexander murmurs, his hand steady at my back.

As we approach, the voices sharpen into words I cannot mistake.

"Rebecca Nurse, you are hereby charged with acts of witchcraft, in league with the Devil," a deputy proclaims, his voice carrying like the toll of a bell. "By order of the magistrates, you are to come with us to answer these charges."

Rebecca stands in the doorway, her silver hair pulled back beneath her cap, horror and grief pouring over her face. Caitie clings to her skirts, wide-eyed with terror.

"No—no, you can't—" My voice bursts out before I think, before I can stop it. I push past the gawking neighbors. "You have no proof. You can't arrest her without evidence, without witnesses under oath. The law requires—"

Dozens of eyes swing toward me. Suspicion sharpens in their gaze like knives drawn from sheaths.

"She thinks she knows much of the law," someone mutters behind me. "Too much, for a maiden so young."

"Sounds like a witch's tongue to me," another shouts.

The words hit like stones. My mouth goes dry, but I force myself to keep speaking, my voice shaking. "You can't simply accuse and bind a woman of her years and faith. This is madness! Where is your writ? Where is your sworn testimony?"

The deputy's face darkens. "Careful, girl. It is not your place to question the court."

Rebecca lifts her chin, calm even as the men step forward with the irons. "Find your peace, Lila," she says softly. "The Lord knows my heart. If He wills me to stand trial, I shall."

Tears sting my eyes. "No! You've done nothing. You've harmed no one!"

But two men seize her by the arms, pulling her from the threshold. Caitie wails, reaching for her grandmother, and my heart breaks at the sound. I lunge forward, only for Alexander's hand to close around my arm, holding me back.

"Lila," he hisses near my ear, low and urgent. "You'll only damn yourself, too."

The crowd is murmuring now, their accusing tones thick with unease. "Strange words… bold tongue… she defends witches."

They're talking about me.

Rebecca meets my eyes as they lead her away, her voice steady despite Caitie's cries. "Be strong, child. The truth will prevail."

But I see the gallows in my mind, stark against the sky, and I know the truth has little place here.

I bite my lip hard enough to taste blood, swallowing the scream clawing up my throat. My fists tremble at my sides, and Alexander's grip tightens, grounding me, holding me still as the world unravels.

Rebecca Nurse is dragged from her home in irons, Salem watches with ravenous eyes, and I feel the noose tighten around my own neck.

GO GET MIRIAM

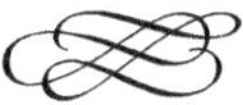

ALEXANDER

ACROSS THE TABLE, my father slices a thick chunk of bread, and Phineas is already pouring broth into his mouth. Mother dabs at her lips with a napkin, her expression tighter than usual, her gaze shifting toward the window as if expecting trouble to peer in. Many women have been arrested over the last few days, among them Rebecca Nurse, Sarah Good, Sarah Osborne, Sarah Wildes, Elizabeth Howe, and Susannah Martin.

I take a deep breath, and try to make cheerful conversation with my family in spite of the gloom looming over us. "The stew is warm and hearty, Mother. Thank you."

"You're most welcome, Alexander," she murmurs. "I was just thinking, and it may not be lady-like to speak of it at supper, but I knew that Sarah Good was with child."

My grip tightens on my spoon. The thought of her, confined in a dark, damp cell in Ipswich, her stomach swollen and empty, chills me. She is no doubt given little to eat or drink, and rest is a luxury she can't afford. My chest tightens with helplessness. How can we call ourselves civilized and godly when a woman carries life inside her and we lock her away?

Father grunts, his brow furrowed. "They've locked up Osborne too, and now little old Rebecca Nurse. It seems there is no end to these unholy acts."

Phineas leans back in his chair. "Even the English family were taken, but I believe they've since been released."

I stare down at my empty bowl, my heart heavy, but then my thoughts shift, reluctantly, to someone else. My voice cuts through the low murmur at the table. "There's someone staying with the Nurse family. Her name is Mistress Lila Bennett. I don't know much about her, but she's… she's a remarkable young woman."

Mother tilts her head, a strand of gray hair catching the candle-light. "Bennett. I don't believe I've heard of her."

"She's beautiful and smart," I say, searching for words that do her justice. "Brilliant, even. And Mother, she's kind. But the way she stood up for Rebecca Nurse yesterday—"

I pause, feeling my chest tighten. "It was nothing short of the most courageous thing I've ever seen. She didn't care what anyone thought at that moment. She only cared about doing what was right."

Father nods slowly, chewing thoughtfully. "She sounds like a good woman, Alexander."

I glance at Mother. She raises an eyebrow, her curiosity piqued. "And what of Elizabeth Booth? I thought you liked her."

I shake my head firmly, almost impatiently. "Mother, I never said that I liked Mistress Booth. She's fine, certainly, but my thoughts, my true feelings are building for Miss Bennett. There's something about her. It's not just bravery, but the steadiness in her, the way she acts without hesitation when it matters. It is quite rare."

Phineas snorts quietly, smirking. "A dangerous thing, getting your heart involved with an outsider in the middle of all this madness."

I try to ignore him, but he's probably right.

Mother murmurs softly, "I hope you know what you're doing, Alexander."

After the meal, I'm deep in thought the whole walk back to my house about the village, my yearning for Lila, and everything in between.

A familiar figure steps out from behind a row of trees, and I pause. "Hezekiah," I say warmly.

Hez falls into step beside me, his expression serious. "Alex, I've heard rumors," he says, his voice low. "People are whispering that Lila Bennett is a witch."

I stop walking, letting the words hang in the twilight air. "Aye. She told me yesterday that she'd heard it, too. At first I thought it would blow over. She hasn't so much as looked at anyone wrong, but now that they've arrested a woman who is with child. They will stop at nothing."

Hezekiah nods. "Aye. I heard enough to make me fear for Lila's safety. And Alexander," he adds, his tone sharp, "I know how you feel about her. I like her, too. She's a good woman. We must help her."

"I know," I say quietly. "I care for her more than I expected, more than I should allow myself to care, given this town and its madness."

"Then we must do something. We can't just wait for them to drag her away."

We walk the rest of the way in a tense silence, the forest swallowing our words. By the time my house comes into view, the sky has darkened, and the first stars prick the heavens. We pause beneath the shadowed limbs of an oak.

"What could we do?" Hezekiah asks, finally. "If it comes down to it, if the magistrates come for her, if the whispers grow too loud…."

I swallow hard, feeling the weight of responsibility settle on my shoulders. "If it comes to that," I say slowly, "there is one thing I need to know. If I were forced to leave this farm, to leave Salem… would you, Hezekiah, be willing to buy it?"

"I've been saving for a farm of my own, and I would hate to see you go, Alex, but if it means saving her… I would understand. You don't have to ask twice if it comes to that."

A lump rises in my throat, but I nod. "No promises, no contracts. Nothing in stone, yet, but if the worst comes, I want to know you would consider it."

Hezekiah gives a firm nod. "Consider it done, friend."

I tighten my cloak around me and motion toward the house. "We should talk inside. It's not safe to linger in the dark with whispers carrying through the village."

Hezekiah falls into step beside me, and together we walk up the lane, shadows long around us. We discuss the details of my land changing hands further, and Hez reminds me that he has a cousin in Boston who runs the city greenhouses and gardens.

"If you move to the city," he says, "you'll be employed within the week."

"Aye. That makes running away from this madness all the more tempting."

Later that night, I lie in bed long after the candles have burned down, but sleep evades me. My mind races, circling over thoughts of Lila—her courage, her wit, the fire in her eyes. I see her face so clearly that it almost hurts.

I care for her more than I have for anyone in my life, and it terrifies and thrills me. Alas, in a town so quick to condemn, to twist a kind word or a helpful deed into proof of witchcraft, love itself can be dangerous. All I want is to keep her safe, to shield her from the cruelty that has swallowed so many others.

By the time the first light touches the horizon, pale and uncertain, I have made my decision. I will go to her. I will see her, speak with her, make sure she is unharmed. The world outside may be cruel and suspicious, but I can at least offer her a measure of safety.

I dress and do the chores quickly. With my horse waiting in the barn, I brush the dust off the saddle and place it on her back with care. I mount and ride with dawn, every heartbeat pounding the urgency in my chest. The path to the Nurse household is familiar, yet the forest feels different in the early light, shadows shifting in ways that set my nerves on edge.

I reach the clearing, and my pulse quickens as I dismount, patting the horse before striding to the front door.

I raise my hand and knock sharply, the sound echoing across the quiet yard. The door swings open, and there she is. Lila carries herself with the same beauty and grace that first drew my attention. Relief washes over me, mingled with a fierce, protective instinct I can't deny.

"Lila," I whisper, stepping closer.

Her eyes meet mine, and I feel every worry, fear, and whispered threat from Salem outside the walls of this clearing fall away, leaving only her. The morning light paints her face, soft and bright. I step closer, and before I can overthink it, I take her hand, lean in, and brush my lips against hers.

"I love you, Lila," I murmur, my voice raw with truth. My forehead rests against hers for a moment, the words tasting of hope, fear, and everything in between.

Her eyes glisten, and she smiles. "I love you too, Alexander," she says, and I feel her words sink deep into me, into the part of me that has longed for something honest, passionate, and certain in a world that is anything but.

We stay like that a heartbeat longer, savoring the promise between us, before the reality of Salem claws its way back in. I brush a strand of hair from her face and sigh as my mind turns back to the chaos surrounding us.

"We need to talk," I say softly, and she nods, sensing the shift. "The arrests… they don't end with Rebecca Nurse. Sarah Good—she's been taken, too. She's in Ipswich's prison, with child, Lila. Can you imagine the conditions in that cell? No proper food, little rest… God knows what they're doing to her."

Her eyes darken, shadows of anger and fear flashing across her face. "We have to help her! We can't let her suffer like this. We need—" Her voice tightens. "We need to go get Miriam. Right now."

I squeeze her hand, steadying both of us. "You're right. We can't waste time. Every second counts for them. We'll go fetch Miriam together."

Her nod is fierce and determined. The world outside may be full of whispers and fear, but for this moment, we are a force of our own.

I pull her close again, pressing a final kiss to her forehead, a silent vow that I will guard her as fiercely as she protects those she loves.

"We need to move fast," she says.

We mount my horse and head for the Carter cottage, and I know, in that instant, that we are no longer simply running from whispers. We are standing against them--together.

MERCY

LILA

ALEXANDER'S HORSE MOVES QUICKLY, its hooves thudding against the dirt path. I cling to the saddle horn with one hand and wrap the other around his forearm. My heart still races from our kiss, but there is no time for romance now.

The thought of Sarah Good, imprisoned and pregnant, fills me with fury. How can anyone call themselves righteous when they allow a woman to suffer so? My stomach twists at the image of her cell—dark, cold, and barely furnished, with food and water rationed, if she receives any at all. She must be frightened, hungry, and desperate. We can't waste a moment. If only I could remember the dates of her baby's birth… and death.

We arrive at Miriam's cottage, and Alexander dismounts first helping me down, his hand placed firmly on my back. I knock more frantically than I mean to, my knuckles rattling the door. Miriam swings it open, her brow furrowed in concern.

"Lila, Alexander," she says, surprise giving way to recognition. "What brings you here so early?"

I step forward, my voice trembling with a mix of fear and determination. "Miriam, Sarah Good has been arrested. She's in Ipswich prison, and she's with child. She's being mistreated, and if we don't act, the baby won't survive."

Miriam's eyes widen, the gravity of the news settling over her. "Ah, yes… it's all happening now," she whispers, pressing her hand to her chest. "That poor woman."

"You know how this ends, Miriam," I say, my voice urgent. "We must go to her now, bring her food, care, whatever she needs. She is depending on us."

Miriam nods, her resolve hardening. "Let me gather some supplies. Alexander, go and borrow a horse from Mr. Woodbury next door. We'll leave immediately."

Alexander and I exchange a glance, relief mingled with tension. "Thank you," I say softly. "Every moment counts."

Miriam moves quickly, mounting the neighbor's horse as I mount behind Alexander, clutching him for balance. The forest falls behind us, the village quiet beneath the early sun. Each stride brings us closer to Ipswich, and closer to the suffering of the innocents that we can't ignore.

Finally, we reach the prison. It looms before us, its gray stone walls grim in the twilight.

We dismount, and Alexander motions for us to stay put while he speaks with the guards. His volume is quiet, but his tone is persuasive. Eventually, I see the flicker of recognition and respect in the guard's eyes. When Alexander nods toward us, Miriam and I step forward.

"Be careful," he murmurs, placing a steadying hand on my shoulder. "Stay close."

I swallow hard and follow her into the dark entryway. The clanging of the iron door behind us makes me flinch. The hall smells of sweat, straw, and urine. Alexander had warned me along our journey, but nothing could prepare me for the stench and the oppressive weight of desperation that hangs like a thick fog in this place.

We find Sarah Good's cell. She sits on the cold, hard floor, her back against the wall and filth and blood surrounding her. The faint cry of an infant reaches me before I see the child, wrapped in a thin, ragged blanket and barely moving.

"Sarah," Miriam says softly, kneeling beside her. "We've come to help."

Sarah lifts her hollow eyes, shadowed and haunted. Relief and despair mingle in her expression. "They said no one would come. I prayed." Her voice breaks, trailing into a hollow cough.

The infant is tiny, fragile, her skin sallow and wrinkled. Sarah rocks her weakly, but the effort seems to sap her completely. A bucket sits in the corner, stained and foul. There is no proper bedding, no warmth, no care beyond what she can provide herself. My stomach churns.

"She's not getting enough to eat," I whisper to Miriam, my voice trembling. "If we don't do something, the baby won't survive."

Miriam's eyes glisten with sorrow. "I know, child. I know. But what can we do?"

I glance around the cell, the guards' occasional footsteps echoing in the corridor. "We have to convince Sarah," I say. "She has to let us take the baby. We can feed her, care for her. She has no chance here."

Sarah's gaze flits between us, wild and frightened. "Her name is Mercy," she whispers. Her voice is hoarse, torn by weeks of fear and malnutrition.

"Mercy needs help," I say, stepping closer. "We won't hurt her. She will survive. Please, trust us, Sarah."

Tears spill down the mother's cheeks, but slowly, she nods, her frail body trembling. Sarah presses a kiss to her baby's cheek and allows Miriam to scoop the infant carefully into her arms. I feel a rush of relief, and yet the danger hasn't passed. We must get her out-- unseen.

We leave the food and healing herbs with Sarah Good, place the baby in the empty basket, covering her lightly with our clean cloth, and make our way out of the prison.

The guards' chatter drifts past the doorway as Alexander's influence holds their attention, allowing us a brief, critical window. Miriam cradles the fragile basket, and I follow close, making sure no one is following us. Every step feels like a lifetime, my pulse a drum in my ears.

Outside, Mercy begins to whimper, and I clutch Alexander's arm instinctively. We have stolen her from the jaws of death, at least for now, but we must get away from this cruel place.

I whisper to Miriam, barely moving my lips. "We have her. Now we must keep her alive."

The responsibility is crushing, but beneath it, a thread of hope winds tight. For the first time, I feel we might actually save someone from this madness.

We ride carefully, the baby now swaddled in my cloak, her tiny body trembling against my chest.

"She won't survive in Salem," I whisper, my voice trembling despite my attempt to stay calm. "Even if we hide her, the town would find a way to harm her, or whoever we chose as her mother. We can't return with her."

Miriam nods. "You're right. We need someone who can nurture her, give her milk, warmth and safety, a sense of community."

I swallow, thinking. "I know the people–the Naumkeag. They are kind, wise, and their children are cherished. Surely there's a mother among them already nursing. She could feed this little one. They will protect her."

Alexander exhales, his hand on the reins. "Then that is where we must go. Do you know how to reach them?"

Miriam nods firmly. "Aye. I can guide us." She leans closer, lowering her voice. "We must move quickly. That baby needs to eat soon."

Finally, we leave the main paths behind, following Miriam's guidance through trails that weave across streams. The horses step lightly over roots and rocks as we press deeper into the woods. I clutch the baby tighter, whispering words of comfort I hope she can hear. "It's all right, little one. You'll be safe soon."

Hours pass in tense silence, the forest thickening around us. When we finally reach the outskirts of the Naumkeag lands, Miriam slows the horse and points toward a clearing ahead.

"They will understand," Miriam assures us. "I will speak to them and explain why we're here."

We dismount carefully, and I take the baby in my arms. I follow Miriam as she calls to the people in their tongue, describing the baby's plight, her premature birth, and the peril she faced in the prison. The Naumkeag listen intently, their expressions softening as the story unfolds.

A mother steps forward, already nursing a child of her own. She reaches for the baby, murmuring gently, and cradles her against her chest. Awe and wonder at the immediate selflessness, kindness, and love floods through me so fully, I have to take a deep breath. Mercy nestles against the woman to nurse, her tiny fingers curling, her cries softening.

I glance at Miriam, whispering, "We did it. She'll survive."

Miriam's eyes glisten with tears. "Yes. We changed her story. Maybe nothing else will go right in this chaos, but this is something good."

Alexander squeezes my shoulder gently, his eyes staying on the baby. "We gave her a chance," he says quietly.

For the first time since leaving Salem, I let myself hope.

We stay the night in the safe and protective Naumkeag village and ride back to Salem at dawn. The baby is safe, swaddled and warm, in the care of the most beautiful and loving people I've ever known.

Naya and I shared an embrace that left me feeling powerful in a way I couldn't fully explain. Even though we can't understand one another's words, her bright smile and beautiful laugh were all I needed to feel certain that leaving the baby there was the right decision. Mercy will grow up safe and loved.

It takes us nearly all day to return, and as we crest the last rise on our journey back to Salem's outer banks, Alexander slows his horse, his hand resting lightly on my shoulder. "That's Proctor's Ledge," he murmurs, his voice low, almost reverent. "And I don't like what I see down there."

I follow his gaze, and my stomach lurches. The gallows rise stark against the fading sun, a rope swaying in the breeze. A crowd has gathered, murmuring, some faces shadowed in the dying light. My chest tightens, my throat constricting.

"We should go another way," Alexander suggests quietly.

Miriam shakes her head, her eyes fixed on the scene below. "No. We need to see who it is they're hanging. Maybe we can stop them. Surely, there's still time."

I nod, even as tears sting my eyes. "We can't just let them kill another innocent woman," I plead.

"You don't understand," Alexander's expression is grim. "You don't want to witness this, Lila. It's Rebecca Nurse."

I feel weak. "No... no, it can't be." The sound escapes me in a strangled whisper.

Anger flares inside of me, hot and deep. I let the tears come freely. "How dare they!" I cry, my voice breaking. "How dare they hang her! An elderly woman! Look at this town, thinking itself pure, thinking itself Christian. Everything in this place is dark--everything is!" I sob, my hands trembling. "And they make it so women can't even care for their own babies! They take life from the innocent... how can this be right?"

Alexander squeezes my hand. "We've done what we could for Mercy. We saved her. Rebecca... we can honor her by standing together, by remembering the truth. That she was a kind and loving woman."

I sniffle, wiping at my tears. "But watching her... taken like this...."

"I know. I know, but right now, we need to get home safely," he reminds me.

"Alexander, I must be here for Rebecca," I insist. "She was like a grandmother to me. I can't let her die alone."

"We can hide in the tree line and pay our respects," Miriam suggests.

Alexander looks to Miriam and then back to me. "We'll leave the horses here and go on foot."

ANYTHING FOR YOU

LILA

WE TIE our horses to low branches and edge along the ridge, the forest masking our presence, until we find a spot where we can witness the brutality without being seen.

The sight makes me want to vomit. Five women stand on the gallows, the ropes around their necks swinging lightly in the breeze. One is my sweet Rebecca Nurse. I know her kind face, her work-worn and yet comforting hands, and her gentle voice. I choke back a sob.

Next to her, I see a figure trembling, her eyes wild with fear. It's Sarah Good. My heart pounds, remembering the baby we saved. She should've been able to raise her baby.

Alexander's voice is low. "That's Sarah Wildes, Susannah Martin, and Elizabeth Howe." His words are like knives. I remember all their names from history books and plays.

Miriam leans closer, her whisper sharp. "Do you see how terrified they are?" Her eyes glisten. "This is murder, plain and simple."

Rebecca Nurse's frail frame is the first. My chest seizes as her body jerks, her neck breaking before she even hits the plank. The sound is a dull crack that makes bile rise in my throat. Another woman kicks wildly, her shoes flying off as her legs thrash against nothing. The rope bites deeper into her throat with every desperate movement. One of them moans, a raw, strangled sound that cuts off in an instant.

I can't breathe. I drop to my knees, my hands clutched over my face, but I can still hear the creak of the ropes as the bodies sway.

We rise from the ridge with stiff knees and heavy hearts, and move toward the horses. The forest seems impossibly quiet after the horror we've just witnessed.

The ride back to Mr. Woodbury's, to return the horse Miriam borrowed, is tense. We move quickly but cautiously, hugging the paths the trees create.

Mr. Woodbury's barn is stacked tall with hay, and Miriam unsaddles his mare. Alexander refills the water bucket and makes sure the mare has enough to eat.

Once the mare is settled, we mount again, Miriam on foot now, me and Alexander on his horse, and follow the forest path back to her cottage.

Alexander steps into her small barn to care for his horse, to brush her down and check the saddle.

Inside Miriam's tiny kitchen, she and I immediately set to work. I fetch the teapot and set water to boil. Miriam moves with fluid precision, filling the kettle and arranging dried herbs for the tea. I kneel beside her, sorting chamomile, mint, and lavender. "Strong enough for comfort," I murmur.

Miriam glances up and nods. "Perfect," she says.

We move in tandem, silent but efficient, our hands busy while our minds still reel from the morning.

Alexander enters finally, damp and smelling faintly of sweat and horses. I glance at him, catching the tension in his shoulders. We sit together, the three of us quiet at first, then Miriam leans forward. "Lila," she says softly, "you can't go back to the Nurse house. Salem will come for you. They already suspect you of witchcraft."

I swallow, nodding. "I agree, but where will I go?"

Alexander places his hand gently on top of mine. "I know it's not proper, and that we've only just met, but you could stay with me until we find something more permanent."

"You'd do that for me, even with all the danger it will bring you if we get caught?"

"I'd do anything for you," he says, and for a moment, I feel the tension in my body relax, if even just a little.

Miriam chimes in. "Then it's settled. You stay with Alexander. He'll protect you."

Later, when shadows darken the roads, Alexander and I lead his horse through the hidden back paths, keeping to the edges, away from watchful eyes, away from judgmental Salem. Every step must be careful, but I feel a sliver of relief. For now, I am safe with Alexander.

When we step inside his house together, I notice the way his jaw tightens and how his movements are stiff, like he's bracing for something.

"Alexander… are you all right?" I ask, stopping in the center of the room.

He swallows hard and finally meets my gaze, his eyes dark and stormy. "I… I don't know," he admits, running a hand through his hair. "Today… seeing them… the women hanged. Five of them. And that tiny baby…." His voice drops, and he hunches over the table, his fists clenched.

I step closer, gently resting a hand on his arm. "I know," I whisper. "It was horrible. But the baby is safe now. They'll take care of her. Even though she looks different from them, she'll grow up loved."

He exhales, meeting my eyes again. "Different… yes. And still, in their eyes, she's just a child. And yet—" He shakes his head. "I keep thinking about her, hoping she'll grow up strong and healthy, that she'll… be happy."

"She will be," I say firmly. "They will treat her with respect. I know it in my heart." There's a pause, heavy in the quiet of the room. I take a breath and ask, "How do you feel… having me here? Hiding in your home? It's dangerous for you, Alexander."

His eyes flash, and I see the simmering fury beneath the exhaustion. "This town," he says, his voice low and hard, "is driving me mad.

I don't care anymore. They could all show up right now, call *me* a witch, and I wouldn't even flinch. I can't abide this evil any longer. It's gnawing at my soul."

I swallow hard and unlace my bonnet, letting my long, dark curls tumble over my shoulders and down my back.

Alexander gasps, and suddenly I feel self-conscious, realizing he has probably never seen a woman his age without her bonnet.

His eyes fill with shock, awe, lust that sends a thrill racing through me. "Lila…" His voice is barely more than a whisper, rough with emotion. "You're even more beautiful than I imagined."

Heat rushes to my cheeks, but I don't look away. Instead, I step closer, letting the warmth of the room, and of him, envelop me. His hand lifts, trembling slightly, to brush a curl from my face, and his fingertips linger.

Then he leans in, and our lips meet, causing everything else to fade. My hands rest lightly on his chest, feeling the warmth and strength beneath my fingers.

When we part, our foreheads still pressed together, I catch the faintest smile tugging at his lips. He studies me, his dark eyes thoughtful, and I can sense him thinking, weighing, savoring the closeness between us. The air hangs electric and thick with emotion until he finally speaks.

"I just realized something. We haven't eaten all day," he murmurs. "I must feed you."

I nod, smiling. "You're right. We can cook something together."

A grin spreads across his face.

We gather bread, cheese, and a few eggs, moving around each other in the kitchen. Our hands brush, and each touch makes a spark. The fire crackles as we work, and soon we sit side by side, sharing the simple meal, warm, quiet, and right.

When the meal is finished, and the fire has dwindled to embers, Alexander looks at me as I'm in the middle of a yawn and says, "You look tired."

"I am," I reply with a sleepy giggle.

"Then you should rest," he murmurs. "You may take the bed. Come, I shall show you."

He leads the way down the narrow hallway, the lantern casting warm light. At the end, he opens the door to a small chamber. A single bed dominates the room, its linen neat and faintly perfumed with lavender.

I step inside, glancing around. "There's… no other bed?" I say.

He hesitates, brow furrowed. "I can take the floor," he offers.

I shake my head. "No, Alexander. It's your bed. Share it with me?"

I step closer and notice a subtle shift in him. His shoulders stiffen, his body tense. I see the way he swallows, his jaw tightening, his eyes dark and focused. He is holding himself back, but I can feel the pull between us, undeniable.

I begin to slowly, teasingly, shed my clothes, letting the layers fall to the floor one piece at a time. I keep my eyes on his, and I can't help but notice the unmistakable evidence of his desire pressing hard against the fabric of his trousers.

I step closer, holding my body to his, and our lips meet in a slow, insistent kiss. He leans in, letting me lead, responding to every movement with hunger.

As our kiss deepens, I unfasten his shirt, running my hands over the firmness of his chest, drinking in the lines of his chiseled abs, sculpted arms, and lean, powerful form.

Every muscle, every taut line seems alive with restraint and need. I sense the heat radiating from him, the thrum of his arousal, and I know that beneath his self-control, he desires me utterly and completely.

"Please, take me, Alexander."

He lifts me effortlessly and carries me to the bed, lying me down gently on the soft linens, and I shiver as his lips brush along my shoulders.

When he explores my breasts with his hands and tongue, I feel my legs naturally part with need. He kneels between my open knees, his hardness brushing against me with his every movement, but he doesn't enter me yet.

Alexander's focus is on my every curve. He cups one breast, rubbing his thumb over my hard nipple while he flicks his tongue over my other. I moan and writhe in ecstasy as he teases every nerve with pleasure.

He reaches down with his fingers to part my wet folds, and I nearly climax from anticipation. "Alexander, I want to feel you inside of me."

I see the passion in his eyes burn even fiercer as he slides inside of me, filling me up perfectly. We move as one, totally attuned, and I never imagined a closeness like this could exist. My body responds to his, our moans mingle in the quiet room, and in that instant, we climax together.

Our hearts beat fast, and I realize this is the first time we've truly shared ourselves so deeply and fully, a moment of love and trust that belongs entirely to us.

I'LL GO WHERE YOU GO

ALEXANDER

I WAKE before the sun fully clears the trees, the soft gray light spilling through the cracks of the shutters. For a moment I don't move. I barely even breathe. Lila is beside me, tangled in the quilt, her hair spread across my pillow like a dark silken halo. She is bare beneath the blanket, bare in my bed, and I should feel shame. Every sermon I've ever sat through told me as much. Yet, I feel completely comfortable, happy, and warm. I feel as if for the first time in my life I'm exactly where I belong.

I ease myself away, careful not to wake her. The floorboards creak under my feet as I dress quickly, pulling on breeches and a shirt. I glance back at her once, half expecting her to stir, but she only sighs in her sleep and curls deeper into the covers. My throat tightens with a mix of wonder and disbelief. A woman, beautiful beyond measure, lies in my bed, and nothing about it seems sinful. It's good and right.

The morning air is humid when I step outside. The yard is damp with dew, and the hens fuss at my approach. I gather their eggs into a wicker basket, whispering calmly so they don't peck my hands, then scatter grain for them and for the goats. Their bleating greets the dawn louder than the birds. I breathe deep, grounding myself in the ordinary chores, though nothing about this place is ordinary any more.

When I return, pushing the door open with my hip, I stop dead. The room is neat, the hearth swept, the table wiped clean. Lila is standing there, clothed now in her modest dress, but her hair still falls loose around her face. She looks like she has always belonged here with me.

"Good morning," she says, her voice refreshing as a summer breeze. She takes the basket from my hands and brushes her lips against my cheek.

My heart stumbles. I can only nod as she turns to the hearth and begins cracking eggs into a pan, humming softly under her breath. I lower myself onto the bench, watching her move with easy purpose, as if tidying and cooking here is the most natural thing in the world. For me it is nothing less than a miracle.

I clear my throat. "I'll need to go into town today."

She glances over her shoulder, her brows raised in question.

"They may have buried the bodies by now," I say quietly. "The women they hanged yesterday. If not, there'll be need for hands to dig graves. And if I'm being completely honest, I want to hear what new tales the people are spinning. Every day the hysteria grows, and I want to make sure they're not going to show up at my family's door. Or at Miriam's. Or here."

Her smile falters, but she nods, sliding the eggs onto a plate and setting it before me. For a breath, I only stare, struck by how whole I feel with her in my kitchen, my house clean, food set before me, the world outside raging but inside here, everything is perfect.

We eat together at the table, the morning quiet except for the scrape of forks and the low crackle of the hearth. When we're done, Lila leans over and kisses me, soft and sure, before rising to clear the plates.

"Be safe while in the village," she says softly.

"I will, but you must stay hidden, Lila. No matter what. Don't open the door if anyone comes, and don't let yourself be seen. Promise me."

She nods. "I promise."

I kiss her once more, then step out. The walk to the village is heavy. When I reach the common, I find Hezekiah already there, standing with his arms folded tight across his chest, looking grim.

"What have they done already this morning? Or are you still as infuriated as I am at what they did last night?"

"They're not digging graves, Alexander," he says, his voice filled with disgust. "The five women they hanged yesterday... they just tossed in a heap by the field. They said if the families want to bury them, they can do it themselves."

The words slam into me. Five women, treated like refuse. "Then we'll bury them," I say without hesitation.

Hezekiah's eyes meet mine, a solemn spark of agreement. Together we join the families already gathered at the field, sheets and carts ready, hovering near the bodies, grief etched deep in their faces.

We help lift each woman carefully, wrapping her in the linen the families brought. I steady the edges of the sheets, guide the carts, and make sure no one falters under the weight. The sight twists my stomach, but I do not look away.

As we dig a grave for Sarah Wildes, villagers stand nearby, not to help, only to whisper. Their voices carry easily, spreading rumors as fast as the bodies are loaded.

"Did you hear? Goody Parker is said to have bewitched her husband into marrying her."

"And young Willie Baker claims the carpenter Samuel Wardwell speaks with the Devil himself. Mark me, they'll hang a man next."

"Oh, that's nothing compared to what I heard about Mistress Lila Bennett. She lives with Rebecca Nurse, and they practiced their witchery together. She's said to be able to conjure up love spells to make any man fall in love with her."

At that, the blood drains from my face, though I keep digging. My hands clench around the shovel so hard my knuckles ache, and yet, they keep talking.

"I saw Lila myself. She was dancing around a fire in the woods, chanting spells."

"The magistrates will have her yet."

I drop my shovel into the dirt with a hard thud and turn to them, my voice sharp as an ax. "Enough! Mistress Lila Bennett is not even here any longer. I took her to Boston yesterday myself. She is there now, far from your prattle. So why don't you keep her name out of your mouths?"

The little knot of gossipers falls silent, their eyes darting, their mouths pressed tight. Hezekiah straightens beside me, shovel in hand, and the weight of our stares is enough to send them scattering.

I return to digging the grave, my chest tight, each strike of the spade into the earth carrying anger and fear. I told them she was in Boston. I hope they believe it. For her sake, they must.

By the time Hezekiah and I finish the grave, the sun is high and my arms ache from the labor. Sweat drips down my temples, and still the anger burns hotter than the work. I wipe my brow, glance at my friend, and say, "Would you like to join me? I need to speak with my family."

He nods, and together we head down the worn path toward my childhood home. The walk is quiet, save for the crunch of gravel beneath our boots and the distant murmur of villagers. My thoughts run faster than my steps. The rumors, the stares, the endless fear–this is no way to live. Not for me, and definitely not for Lila.

Mother opens the door when we arrive, her apron dusted with flour, a faint smile softening when she sees me. Father is at the table mending a wooden yoke, and Phineas sits by the hearth, a long leg stretched out, whittling a stick with his knife.

I nod to them, motioning for Hezekiah to follow me inside. "I've something I must tell you."

Phineas looks up first, his boyish face creasing with curiosity. "You sound like you've more bad news."

I take a breath, steadying myself. "I'm thinking of leaving Salem."

Father sets down the yoke, his eyes narrowing, not in anger but in consideration. Mother listens intently, folding her hands in front of her.

"I'm weary of this place," I continue, my voice low but firm. "Of the trials, the gossip, the fear in every corner. It is not living anymore.

It feels like choking. I want something different. I told Hezekiah I'd sell him my land since Phin has his own inheritance waiting for him already."

The room stays quiet longer than I can bear. At last, Mother exhales softly. "I can't say I blame you, son."

Her words shock me more than her silence. She meets my gaze with weary eyes. "I don't like what this town has become either. I see neighbors whispering, turning on one another. It is no place for peace."

Father nods slowly, running a hand over his graying beard. "I never thought I'd see the day you'd want to go, Alexander." He leans back in his chair. "But I understand. And if you do leave, you'll have no reproach from me."

Phineas finally speaks, his voice quiet but sharp. "If you leave, you'll take me with you, won't you? I don't want to stay here, either."

My chest tightens. He's still so young, and yet the darkness of Salem has touched him, too. I place a hand on his shoulder. "We'll see, brother. We'll see."

The air in my parents' house grows heavy with talk of leaving, of selling, and of change. At last I rise, resting a hand briefly on Mother's shoulder, then Father's. "I'll be back soon, but for now, I must get home."

Phineas follows me to the door, trailing like a shadow, his eyes bright with questions he doesn't yet speak. I ruffle his hair like I used to when he was smaller and promise, "We'll talk more soon."

Outside, Hezekiah falls into step beside me. We walk the long path together, the quiet broken only by birdsong and the low whistle of the wind through the trees. At length, I say, "I meant it. If you want the land, I'd rather it be yours than left to strangers."

Hezekiah studies me, his jaw tight. "I'll purchase it from you if and when you decide."

We clasp hands firmly before our paths split. "Until tomorrow," I say.

"Until tomorrow," he says, heading down the lane toward his family's farm.

I turn homeward, the magnitude of the day pressing on my shoulders. Yet, when I push open my door, the sight before me melts every burden away.

The hearth is lit, casting a soft glow across the room. The table is set with a simple meal, steaming and deliciously fragrant. Beside it, a basin of warm water waits, a folded cloth resting neatly on the side. Lila stands there, her eyes sparkling when she sees me, her lips curving into the smile that has undone me since the first moment I saw it.

"You're back," she says softly, crossing the room to press a kiss to my lips.

"I am." My voice is rough but steady. She smells of lavender, and when her arms slip around me, I feel loved in a way I never have.

She guides me to the basin, dips the cloth, and hands it to me so I can wash away the dirt and sweat of the day. It is such a simple gesture, yet it strikes deep. No sermon, no law, no man's word could ever convince me that this is wrong.

Over supper, we share a quiet, pleasant meal. The simple act of sitting together, eating in peace after the past few days, makes me certain of something I never dared to imagine before. Lila is my home. She's where I belong.

When the plates are cleared, I reach for her hand. "Lila," I begin, "what would you think of moving to Boston, of leaving Salem behind, starting anew there?"

Her eyes search mine, and she squeezes my hand, a smile curving her lips. "I'll go where you go, Alexander."

In this moment, I know that she is the one, and my future is with her.

BELIEVE ME

LILA

THE CHORUS of morning drifts in from outside–hens clucking, goats bleating, the scrape of boots and hooves on gravel as Alexander tends the animals. I lie in bed, listening. It's my second morning here, in his home, and yet already it feels safer than anything I've known in Salem. It is safer than any corner I've hidden in these last weeks, and safer than any breath I've drawn while the villagers' eyes turned toward me with suspicion.

I pull the quilt around me and take a slow, calming breath. The world outside is still dangerous, and still cruel. I've been accused, labeled a witch, gossiped about in public places, and stared at with distrust. Yet, here in Alexander's house, I can be invisible if I need to, unseen and unharmed.

Sliding from the bed, I pull on my dress, my hands shaking slightly as I move to the kitchen, not from cold, but from the gravity of what I am about to do.

I fill a small kettle from the water pot and move to the herbs Alexander keeps in his windowsill garden: chamomile, mint, and lemon balm. I line them up along the counter and begin preparing tea, letting the familiar motions anchor me.

Yesterday, I baked bread, boiled water, made Alexander's dinner from scratch, and I'm relieved Rebecca Nurse and her daughter taught me the skills necessary to survive in this era. The lessons carry me through moments like this, when I can be of some assistance to Alexander.

He'll bring in eggs from the hens soon, and I'll cook them. It is the ordinary rhythm of life, and yet my mind is far from ordinary this morning. The truth I carry presses against me, insistent and unavoidable. I'm from another time, a future he can't imagine. If he doesn't believe me, if he thinks me a witch, or if he turns away in fear or anger….

I set the tea and plates on the table, my hands trembling. I could flee, hide in the shadows forever, and be safe, but I know I can't do that if we're to have any chance of a life together. If he truly intends to take me to begin a new life in Boston, he deserves to know the truth about me. I have decided to tell him, but I'm terrified.

The door creaks open, and I glance up just as Alexander steps inside, his boots dusted with gravel, the morning sunlight catching his sandy hair. Relief twists with fear in my chest, but he smiles at me, and it feels… safe. He always looks so genuinely happy to see me.

"Good morning," he says, lifting a small basket of eggs, handing it to me with a quiet nod.

"Good morning, and thank you for letting me rest," I whisper, setting the eggs on the counter.

"Of course," he says, kissing my temple. "You're just as beautiful when you're asleep."

I feel my cheeks flush at his flirtation but begin cracking eggs into the pan. My thoughts are whirling, but I force myself to focus.

"Alexander," I say, my voice tight. "There's something I must tell you. It's very serious."

He tilts his head, his brow drawn in curiosity. "You have my ear."

I set the plates in front of us, the eggs golden and steaming. Alexander slides into the chair across from me, and I take my seat. I draw in a breath, the words heavy on my tongue. "What I'm about to tell you is going to sound like complete nonsense and like I'm jesting, but I promise you I'm not. What I'm going to tell you is completely true. I'm not from this time. I'm from the future, from the twenty-first century."

His fork pauses mid-air. "The future?" he asks, his eyes filled with intrigue. Skepticism and caution ripple through him, but the warmth in his gaze doesn't waver.

"I'm from Salem. I grew up here, just not in your time," I continue, my hands clenching the edge of the table. "I grew up here, but in the year 2025. I knew everything that has happened so far would transpire, and I know everything that will happen with the witch trials. I've read the records, acted out the trials and gallows scenes in plays, read about them in books, and studied the history. Alexander, I knew that Sarah Good's baby would be born in prison. That's why I had to act to save her. In my time, that baby died in the prison. We changed history when we saved her life."

Alexander's fork falls with a clatter onto his plate. He leans back, his eyes searching mine. "You traveled backward in time?"

I nod. "I did, and I know the names, the events. I can't remember all the dates, but I know who will die, and I know how tragically it will all end."

He is silent for a long moment, taking in my words. Then he reaches across the table, placing his hand over mine. His touch is warm and comforting. "If what you say is true, then you carry a burden I can scarcely imagine."

I exhale, trembling with both relief and fear. "It is… it is heavier, and more terrifying than anything I've ever known."

He rises, crossing to me, takes my hand, and lifts me into a gentle hug. "Lila," he says softly, pressing his lips to my forehead. "This must be an unimaginable weight to bear. Yet, you are here, and I will share it with you. We'll carry it together. You're not alone. I swear it."

"You believe me?"

"Of course. You're a good and honest woman. You have no reason to lie about something like this, especially when speaking these words could bring you trouble. There have been moments since I met you when I wondered at the strange words or phrases you've used. I recall times when you spoke of events as if they had already happened, or remembered things that hadn't yet come to pass. Everything you're telling me now… it makes perfect sense, in a world where suddenly nothing else seems to make sense at all."

"Thank you, Alexander. You have no idea how relieved I am to be believed."

Our lips meet, soft at first, then with more urgency, hands tangling in each other's hair and clothing. Each kiss pulls us closer, a rush of heat and need that makes it impossible to think. We stumble backward, caught in the pull of each other, and the next thing I know, Alexander is guiding me toward the bedroom, both of us laughing and gasping between kisses as the door closes quietly behind us.

He pulls me close, his hands lingering over me, his lips tracing a path from my face down my neck, each touch sending shivers through me. We move together, desperately undressing and pressing against each other, lost in the warmth and safety of our closeness.

He pauses, his forehead resting against mine, his eyes searching mine for permission. "May I kiss your most intimate parts, your beautiful, delicate flower?" he asks softly.

My heart races, and I nod, leaning in. "Only if you want to," I breathe, and the air between us shimmers with lust.

Alexander kisses down to my belly button and then trails kisses up and down my inner thighs. When he stops just above my slit, I'm already dripping wet. His mouth works over me, and I close my eyes, tipping my head back and holding my breath.

It only takes him a few moments to bring me over the edge as I writhe and cover my mouth, trying to muffle screams of delight.

He pauses, his eyes searching mine as if trying to read my thoughts. "I've… never done anything like that before," he admits, his voice low.

I laugh softly. "That's almost as unbelievable as the fact that I'm from another century," I tease.

He laughs at my joke, but I'm already pulling his trousers the rest of the way off so that I can pull him down on the bed next to me. I kiss his lips and taste myself on them, as I stroke his hardness.

When I climb on top of him, and slide onto his throbbing cock, he lifts his head, gasping. I begin riding him in slow rhythm, grinding my sensitive bud against his shaft, enjoying every moan that escapes his lips even more than my own pleasure. His cock is perfect, and fills me so completely. When I begin to feel myself clenching around him, he feels it too, and we crash into euphoria together.

We collapse against each other, and I rest my head on his chest, feeling his strength beneath me.

"I love you, Lila," he whispers, his voice heavy with emotion.

"I love you, too, Alexander," I answer, letting my gaze linger on his face, memorizing every line.

For a long moment, we simply stay like that, our hearts slowing, words unnecessary. The danger outside, the accusations, none of it matters here.

All that exists is Alexander and me, and the truth of what we feel.

GOD WILL JUDGE YOU

ALEXANDER

I WALK BESIDE HEZEKIAH, our boots crunching over the dirt road leading toward Giles Corey's farm. Lila is home, tending the house, and though her presence is a comfort, I can't shake the gnawing unease in my chest.

The village is unraveling. Each day brings a new accusation, a new arrest. Mothers tremble as their children whisper of witches, and men look at one another with suspicion instead of friendship.

"He's stubborn, you know," Hezekiah mutters, breaking the silence. His breath curls in the cold air. "Giles won't yield to them easily."

I nod, thinking of the man's face, the lines carved by years of toil and defiance. Giles Corey has always been a man of principle, and that's what makes the accusations against him all the more dangerous. "He's proud," I reply. "Too proud to bend, too honest to lie."

The Corey house comes into view against the pale winter sky. Smoke drifts lazily from the chimney. Giles is outside, sitting in his rocking chair on the porch.

"Mr. Corey," I call to him, raising a hand in a friendly wave.

"Good morning, Alexander," he greets us with a tip of his hat. "Hezekiah."

As we approach, I must force my chest to calm. "We've come to speak with you," I say carefully, "about your situation in Salem. You know the villagers are becoming more desperate. The accusations are flying faster than any man can track them, and for some baffling reason, the court listens to every word."

Giles' jaw tightens. "Aye," he says. "I hear my name in the whispers. They want my land, lads. It's as simple as that, and you know they'll have to hang me in order for my children to get my land. I've made my peace with the Lord above, and I'm ready to go."

Hezekiah glances at me, then back at Giles. "What do you mean, sir?"

He looks at us, his eyes narrowing, but I see no fear, only the stubborn resolve I've always respected. "If I plead guilty, they'll take my land. If I tell them that I'm no witch and no one in this town has ever been a witch, they'll hang me, and then my children will still be able to inherit my land. These foolish trials, this utter nonsense, will not bend me to their whims. I'll speak no falsehoods… not for fear, not for mercy."

I swallow hard, the weight of his words crashing over me. "Mr. Corey, you are perhaps the most courageous man I've ever had the pleasure of knowing."

"Aye," Hez chimes in. "And you are a far more faithful servant of the Lord than I, my good man."

Giles nods once and goes back to rocking again, the rhythm of the chair punctuating the silence. The sun rises higher, but the light seems brittle, failing to pierce the shadow of dread settling over Salem.

I return to the house, the summer heat clinging to my clothes. Lila is at the table, her hands wrapped around a mug of tea. The moment I step inside, I sense something has changed, and there's an edge in her gaze I can't ignore.

"Lila?" I ask, setting my hat on the rack. "What is it?"

She exhales slowly, unease melting over her expression. "Alexander… it's Giles Corey," she says, her voice trembling. "I know what the court plans for him, and I'm not sure how to tell you this, but he will not be hanged."

I freeze. "What do you mean? That's good news, isn't it?"

Her fingers tighten around her cup. "No, Alexander, they don't spare his life. He… they intend to press him to death. They'll lay stones on his chest. He'll endure hours of agony. It will take him three days to die."

I force myself to fight back tears. "They can't." I choke on the words. "He's a good man… he'll—"

"I'm sorry, Alexander. I've read the accounts. All you can do is brace yourself for the horror to come."

I sink into a chair, staring at the table, feeling the tug of helplessness and guilt within. Lila reaches across, placing her hand over mine.

The thought of Giles, so strong of spirit yet so fragile of body–Salem has become nothing but a place of shadow and fear. Mr. Corey, a man I respect more than any, is poised for a fate worse than death.

A FEW DAYS LATER, THE COURT CONVENES AGAIN IN SALEM. I FOLLOW Hezekiah and Phineas through the throng of villagers, whispers and stares cutting at us from every side. The hysteria grows with each passing day, and I fear for the steadfast Giles Corey more than anyone.

As we enter the meeting house, my stomach churns. Giles sits at the defendant's table. His eyes find mine for a fleeting moment, undaunted, unshaken. Pride and dread twist in my chest.

The judge clears his throat. "Giles Corey, you are accused of witchcraft. How do you plead?"

Giles lifts his chin, his voice steady, carrying across the silent courtroom. "I stand mute, Your Honor. I will give no answer."

A murmur ripples through the crowd.

"Do you refuse to enter a plea?" the judge presses.

"I refuse," Giles says simply, eyes unwavering. "I will not speak falsely. My silence shall stand, and my estate will pass to my children, not be claimed by the court."

Hezekiah mutters under his breath, awed rather than critical. "The bravest man I've ever known," he says quietly.

"I am aware of the consequences," Giles continues, his voice firm. "Yet, I endure, that my family may be secure. Better to die in truth than to live by lies and see my land taken from my sons."

A hush settles over the courtroom. Even the judge hesitates for a moment, as if the courage of one frail, God-fearing man has penetrated the mindlessness of the court.

"Then it is as you choose," the judge finally says, his voice tight. "Remain silent, and you shall not be hanged like the others. Instead, you will face *peine forte et dure*—pressed under heavy stones until you either answer or die."

A collective gasp rises from the crowd. Some villagers clutch their mouths. Others stumble back in shock.

Hezekiah mutters, his voice low, "By God... they can't mean it."

Giles doesn't flinch. "I will not speak. Let the stones fall. Let God witness the truth of my heart," he says, each word deliberate, refusing to bow.

Phineas nudges my arm, his voice low. "Alexander... *pressed*? What is it?"

I glance at him, uncertain how to explain. Hezekiah leans in. "It's called *peine forte et dure*. Heavy stones are laid upon the accused, bit by bit, until he speaks—or dies. A man like Giles, proud and unyielding... it's the punishment they use when a plea is refused."

Phineas's face tightens. "They actually crush a man to force him to answer?"

Hezekiah nods grimly. "It's a method the court will use to make an example of a stubbornly brave man like Giles Corey, fearmongering to keep the rest of the village in line."

I clutch Hezekiah's sleeve as the magistrate explains that we, and a handful of other men–those the court deems responsible and trustworthy, must witness the procedure. Among them, I recognize

Constable William Stoughton and Giles's own neighbors, who have already signed confessions against him. We are to see that justice is served, the law followed… though it twists the stomach and chills the blood. Mr. Corey is remanded to the prison, and Hez and I follow as witnesses, thankfully sending Phineas home.

Giles is placed upon the bare floor of a low, dark chamber. Naked, save for the decency the law grudgingly allows, the oldest, frailest man I have ever seen lies down as the sheriff and attendants begin their grim preparations. Stones, some small, some large, are stacked beside the hatchway overhead.

Giles lifts his eyes toward us, unbroken, unbowed. Even in this state, eighty years etched into every sinew, he stares with the stubborn pride of a man who has tilled his land, raised his children, and dared the harshness of life to bend him.

The attendants begin, lifting the first stones and lowering them with deliberate cruelty. The old man groans beneath the weight, his body shuddering under the unrelenting pressure, but he speaks no word.

"He won't plead," Hezekiah whispers, his jaw tight, his knuckles white. "He will not bend. God help him."

I can hardly breathe. My chest aches, as if the weight of the stones presses upon me as well. Phineas would have fainted if he were here, and I can barely stand the sight. Giles's body creaks, fragile under the accumulation, his labored breaths rasping. The attendants keep pace, piling more weight atop him, until finally, I find my voice. "You who are gathered here," I call to the people pressed along the wall, "you bear witness to cruelty, to the work of human hands acting in fear! You are vile, disgusting, and God will judge you all for this!"

Hezekiah steps beside me, his voice loud and trembling. "Turn from this evil! Repent before the Lord, for this man's death is your condemnation!"

We don't linger. The three days that will stretch before Giles–the hunger, the thirst, the stones, are more than any mortal man should endure, and neither I nor Hezekiah can stand to watch. We leave the small chamber, our hearts heavy, our legs shaking, as the murmurs of the crowd trail behind us.

The stones continue their relentless descent, and Giles's defiance echoes silently into the dark.

CHOICES

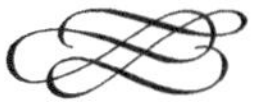

LILA

THE SMELL of wheat pancakes and maple syrup clings to the air as I sit across from Alexander at the table.

"We could be gone within a week or two, if we choose to move to Boston," Alexander says.

Boston would bring us safety, distance, and the chance to breathe. We could begin a life together, free of the death, pain and chaos of Salem.

"Are you certain you want to leave your farm, and your family, Alexander? Eventually, the witch trials will end, your village will go back to normal, and you will be safe. Your family doesn't face suspicion. None of you will be harmed, but if you sell your farm to Hezekiah and move to Boston just for me—"

"Aye," he interjects. "I am certain. I will do anything and everything to ensure your safety. Even after the accusations end and the village tries to go back to how it was before all of this madness, there will never be peace here again… only grief, only suspicion. This is nowhere to raise a family."

Family. The word echoes in my mind. Of course, Alexander will want me to mother a family. Am I ready for that? Just weeks ago, I was a law student in the twenty-first century preparing to become a lawyer, and now I'm facing a life as a wife and mother in the 1600s. I must not only decide whether to follow Alexander to Boston, but also whether to abandon any hope of returning to *my* time.

Alexander reaches for my hand across the table. "At least in Boston you'll be safe. No one knows us there. No one will whisper your name as they pass."

I nod, though my heart aches.

"I've errands in the village. I'll only be gone a short while." He rises and places his hand on my shoulder, a warmth I want to sink into and never leave.

When the latch falls behind him, the house feels too large, too hollow. I can't stay in Salem. I know that much with a clarity that makes my skin prickle. The walls close in on me here. Every footstep outside is a threat, every knock a noose. I have seen too much death already, and I can't be next.

I don't know which I want more: to find my way home to 2025, to the life I lost, or to gamble everything on Boston and a life with Alexander.

I push away from the table at last and carry the dishes to the basin. My hands find the rhythm of work almost without thought: scrape, rinse, stack. The rough ceramic clinks faintly, and I tell myself that if I keep busy, the questions spinning in my head will quiet.

They don't.

Stay, go. Hide, speak. Be Alexander's good wife, and bear him children, or reach for something more, even here in a world that doesn't want me to be more than a wife and mother.

I picture Boston in its infancy–ships crowding the harbor, bustling streets, and new beginnings. Could I find a foothold there? Could I carve out some place where I am more than a wife? Certainly they'd never let me learn law, let alone become a practicing lawyer, based on my gender alone.

The cloth in my hand grows damp and cold as I scrub the table. I imagine myself standing on a Boston street, a book of law clutched in my arms, and men staring, laughing, and shaking their heads. A woman who wants to plead cases and make arguments for justice… would they drag me to the stocks before I could even speak?

I think of Miriam. She's the only one who knows the truth of time's strangeness. She slipped through time just like me. If anyone could understand the desperate thrum of wanting to go back, it's her. Do I dare ask? What if she knows a way back, and what if the answer is something I can't bear?

I glance at the door, at the heavy latch Alexander reminded me to keep bolted. Even locked, it feels like the village is breathing down my neck. Salem doesn't let me forget where I am.

For a moment, I let myself wonder, what if happiness is simpler than I think? Just me and Alexander, in a place in the city where no one knows us. A marriage, children, the ordinary rhythm of life. He loves me. I love him. Why isn't that enough?

But I've always wanted more. The truth settles, heavy and undeniable. I love him, but I also love the woman I was: the student, the dreamer, the fighter. If I give that up, am I still me?

I'm mid-daydream when there's a sudden knock at the door, causing me to flinch, and then freeze. I dart my eyes to the door, then to the windows. No one is supposed to know I'm here. If they find me….

The silence stretches, and I begin to sweat through my dress, fear knotting in my gut.

Please don't let them know I'm here.

Finally, I hear footsteps retreating, the floorboards creaking on the porch. I force myself to take a breath and move, tiptoeing to the window. Peering out, I catch the edge of a bonnet vanishing down the path. Whoever she is has left a basket on the porch.

I wait, straining to hear if anyone's around before I unbar the door. I lift the basket inside, warm against my palms, the smell of fresh bread rising to meet me.

Tucked among the loaves and sweet cakes is a folded slip of parchment, tied with a neat ribbon. My throat tightens as I read Elizabeth Booth's words thanking Alexander for his kindness, wishing him strength.

I set the note down, staring at it. My stomach twists, a tangle of jealousy and terror. To Elizabeth, Alexander is a free man, untethered. What would she think if she knew he'd given his heart to me? She'd probably have me arrested before the bread cooled.

By the time Alexander returns, the light outside has shifted golden, sinking toward evening. He sets down his satchel, and his eyes go straight to me. "Something smells good in here."

I clear my throat, forcing casualness. "Someone left you a basket of bread and cakes. I think you have an admirer."

His brows lift, a boyish grin breaking through the weariness on his face. "Let me guess. Elizabeth Booth?"

I can't help the sigh that slips out. "And you find that amusing, do you?"

He chuckles, shaking his head as he loosens his boots. "The whole village knows she has a soft spot for me. Don't worry about that. You know I love you."

I stare at him, my arms folded across my chest. "Alexander, she accused me of witchcraft not so long ago. She's not exactly my favorite person."

That wipes the smile from his lips. He steps closer, his hands brushing down my arms. "I didn't mean to make light of it. Forgive me."

I nod, but the melancholy remains, pulling at me. He notices, of course he does. His gaze softens. "You seem far away tonight, Lila. Is it Elizabeth that troubles you?"

"No. It's not just that. Would you… would you invite Miriam for supper? I can't very well go to her house myself, and I would just really like to speak with her about an important matter. It's safe to tell her I am here."

He studies me, puzzled, but nods at once. "Of course. If you're certain, I'll fetch Mistress Carter if it pleases you."

When the door shuts behind him again, my chest loosens. I busy myself preparing stew, slicing the bread, and arranging the table with more care than necessary. It soothes me, knowing Miriam will be here soon.

When Alexander returns with her, relief crashes over me the moment our eyes meet. I rush forward, wrapping her in a tight hug. "Miriam."

She squeezes me just as fiercely. "Miriam, I have told Alexander only my own secrets. He knows the secret I told you, that I'm from the future," I say.

"I had imagined it would only be a matter of time before your trust in each other grew enough for you to tell him," she replies with a smile, her green eyes sparkling.

We sit, the three of us gathered around the small table. For a few moments, we try to make pleasant small talk, but I can't keep my question inside forever.

I lay my spoon down, my pulse racing. I glance at Alexander. "Please understand. I love you, Alexander, and the question I'm about to ask Miriam is not a doubt of my love for you. But I had a life before this. I was going to be a lawyer. I belonged to another world, another time. It's safer there, freer for women. And well…."

I look at Miriam now. "I just need to know if it's even possible. If I wanted to, could I ever get back?"

Alexander's hand tightens around mine. He doesn't speak, only waits, his thumb brushing comfort over my knuckles.

Miriam puts down her slice of bread, her eyes locked on mine. Her voice is gentle, sure. "Lila, you will undoubtedly return to your own time at some point. The choice will be yours whether you stay there, or whether you come back here."

LOVE IS ENOUGH

ALEXANDER

LILA MIGHT LEAVE me and go back to the life she came from, the one I'll never be able to reach. My stomach twists, heavy and cold, as if a stone has settled there. I grip the edge of the table, my knuckles white, trying to steady myself while my mind races.

"Hold on a minute," I say, my voice tight. "Miriam... forgive me, but how do you know all this?"

Miriam's confidence doesn't waver. She inclines her head slightly as if expecting this exact question. "Alexander, I am only telling you this because I know that you are a good, kind, and free-thinking man," she says, soft but firm. "Lila is not the only one from another time. I, too, am from the future. Not only that, but I am a true witch."

I laugh before I even realize it, a short, disbelieving bark of laughter. "You jest. Truly? This... witchcraft nonsense? Not from you too, Miriam."

My eyes dart between the two women. The hysteria sweeping through Salem is one thing, but this folly is something else entirely. Lila's expression holds concern, and I realize they are serious. My laughter dies in my throat.

Miriam tilts her head, as if my incredulity is expected. "I am telling the truth, Mr. Paine," she says. "I am a witch, yes, but not in the way you think. I do no harm. I heal. I understand time, nature, and energy in a way others either can't… or that they choose to ignore."

I shake my head, still reeling, and Miriam continues. "I was born and raised here in Salem in the middle of the twentieth century. My ancestors are from here. Some live in this town even now. I know the land, herbs, rivers, ocean, caverns, and the powerful energies. I know how to move between ages, but I am *not* the witchy villain you have been taught to fear."

My mind races. All those accusations, all the fear and hatred flooding Salem, and now it turns out that nothing and no one is ever as they seem.

"I teach and guide when I can. Lila will return to her time. That is not her choice to be questioned, but in the end, she may choose to remain here, with you, if her heart so wishes."

I take a deep breath, trying to absorb it all. I glance at Lila, and my chest aches with both fear and longing.

After dinner, I escort Miriam home. The village streets are quiet, dimly lit by lanterns that sway in the gentle wind. I can't stop thinking about Lila's words, her eyes, the way she had laid her heart bare tonight.

"She is worth it, Alexander," Miriam says. "Anything good is worth the work, the wait, and the patience it takes to fight for each other. Just stick by her. I have every faith in the two of you."

I glance at her, startled by the certainty in her tone. "How can I possibly live up to the life she deserves? How can I hold on to someone who doesn't even truly belong in my century? Her world before me was safer, brighter, more alive. The way she describes it all… she misses it. I know she does."

Miriam looks up at me as we arrive at her gate. "Alexander, the fact that you even asked that question," she says, and a small smile tugs at her lips, "proves you are a good man. You love her. True love is always enough."

"Thank you, Miriam, for your wisdom, and your friendship."

She gives me a slight curtsey, bids me farewell, and turns to step inside her front garden.

As I walk back through Salem, the familiar streets are empty under the night sky, and I can't believe what has become of this place. People accusing one another of witchcraft, neighbors betraying neighbors, fear so thick it chokes the air, and yet there is truth, too. A real witch walks among us, kind and wise. I can't reconcile the world I once knew with the one I live in now.

My thoughts drift back to Lila—the fire in her eyes, the determination she carries, the laughter she hides behind a careful mask. How can anyone expect her to settle quietly into this century, when the world she left behind is so much better for her? How can I even ask her to? I swallow hard. Perhaps it is selfish to hope she stays, but what choice do I have? My heart is hers, whether she remains or returns to her own time.

I wonder about Boston and the life we might build there, a place where no one knows our names, where we might be safe, where we could breathe together. But the more I imagine it, the heavier the doubt becomes. She might not stay. She might return to the life she left behind, and if she does, what am I left with? A memory? Certainly. A broken heart? Forever.

The familiar silhouette of my house grows near. My legs feel heavy, and my chest tightens with a mixture of awe and despair. Lila, the woman of my dreams, the one I would move mountains for, might not belong here at all. I pause on the doorstep, staring at the warm glow behind the glass, and my heart aches in ways I cannot name.

The moment I step inside, the familiar scent of home does little to calm the storm inside me. Lila sits at the table, her hands folded as if waiting for me. I don't hesitate. I cross the room in two long strides, and before she can react, I take her face in my hands and press my lips to hers.

It's a kiss born of desperation, relief, and a thousand unspoken words. She leans into me, her hands finding mine. The world beyond these walls—Salem, Boston, centuries, time itself—vanishes.

I pull back just enough to see her face. "Lila," I whisper, my voice trembling. "Whatever you decide, whatever path you take, you must know this: I will love you forever."

She swallows, her lips parted, her voice a soft tremor. "Alexander, I don't know what I should do. I don't know if I belong here or there. Sometimes, I feel like I don't belong anywhere at all."

I tighten my hold on her hands, shaking my head. "Even if centuries separate us, I will love you through it all."

Her brow furrows, a mixture of fear and longing in her eyes. "And if I go back?" she whispers. "If I leave, will you still think of me?"

"Always."

She leans into me, resting her forehead against mine. "I love you so much, Alexander."

I brush a strand of hair from her face, memorizing the curve of her cheek. "We'll take it one day at a time. Tonight, I'll hold you. Tomorrow... we face whatever comes, together or apart, but know this: nothing will change how I feel about you."

Her hands tighten on mine, and she whispers, "Thank you for letting me decide for myself, for loving me no matter what."

I gather her in my arms and guide her gently toward the bedroom. "Sleep well, my love," I murmur.

I hold her as she drifts off, willing the night to stretch long and safe, wishing I could hold time itself at bay.

In the morning, the sun is high and hot, baking the dirt paths as I tend to the animals. Sweat slicks my back, and the smell of hay clings to my skin. I'm brushing down the mare when I hear a commotion nearby.

I straighten, my ears straining. At first, I think it's a quarrel among neighbors, but the panic in the shouts twists something in my gut. I mount the mare and give her the signal to run up the road.

I see Mary Parker, my neighbor and lifelong friend, being dragged from her house by a cluster of constables. Mary fights with every ounce of strength she has, her fists pounding, her voice raw with terror and anger.

This is a woman I've known since childhood. She tended her family, raised her children and grandchildren, and kept the village afloat in quiet ways. Now she's being treated like a criminal, accused without reason.

I step forward, my boots stirring dust, and shout, "Mary! Stop! Leave her be!" My voice cracks with sorrow and disbelief.

Some townspeople glance at me. Others shrink back, unwilling to interfere. The constables, methodical and merciless, keep hauling her and other women down the street toward the meetinghouse. Mary fights them every step, shouting curses and defiance. My chest tightens, rage and helplessness twisting together.

I want to charge them, to tear her from their grasp, but even I know the limits of my strength against a group like this. Still, I ball my hands into fists, and I can't tear my eyes away. Mary looks at me, desperation in her eyes, and it makes the fire in my chest burn hotter.

By God, Salem is a town gone berserk. I will not be part of this madness any longer, this vile village, with its whispers, accusations, and executing of the innocent. This place has nothing left for me. If there is a future worth building, it will be somewhere far from these streets and this suffocating fear.

WITCHY WOMAN

LILA

I WAKE TANGLED in Alexander's arms, his chest warm against mine. He moves, pressing closer, and I arch into him without thinking. Our fingers lace, tightening in a conversation that needs no words. I feel his lips at the curve of my neck, soft and teasing, and I laugh against him, a sound low and content. "Good morning," I murmur.

"Good morning," he replies as he nuzzles my shoulder.

I roll over and brush my lips across his, the only invitation he needs. His arms close around me, pulling me against him, and I feel the familiar spark ignite between us. He kisses me deeply, hungrily, until the rest of the world dissolves.

The morning light spills through the shutters as our bodies move together, the rhythm unhurried, intimate, every touch speaking of trust as much as desire. His breath is warm against my neck. My fingers explore his chest and biceps as I ride him, grinding against him in pure bliss.

When he reaches up and squeezes my breasts, I'm thrown over the edge of climax, hard and satisfying. My reaction to the pleasure he brings me drives him on, until at last he gives in, surrendering to the same storm of pleasure.

Finally, after recovering in one another's arms, I find my voice again. "We should get up," I say with a soft laugh. "Breakfast won't make itself."

He groans, stretching, hand still in mine. "Five more minutes," he says, but I shake my head, tugging him to his feet.

The kitchen smells of smoke and fresh bread when I set bowls on the table. Alexander stirs the porridge, his eyes glancing at me, still carrying the heat and aftershocks of our morning tryst.

"I have decided to begin the plans today to move us to Boston," he says finally, his voice low, testing the word as if tasting it for the first time. "A new start. Away from Salem, from all the madness."

"I would feel much safer there. Thank you, Alexander."

"I'll handle everything. We'll make it work. We'll carve out a life there together."

After breakfast, Alexander heads toward Hezekiah's house. I watch him through the window, my chest tight with a mixture of longing and relief. He has plans now, practical steps to carve out a future for us, and the weight of it makes me feel both hopeful and anxious.

I turn back to the kitchen, broom in hand, sweeping the scattered crumbs. The dust rises in pale motes in the warm light, the rhythm of the broom almost meditative, though my thoughts refuse to settle–Boston, Salem, my place in either, and what Miriam meant when she said I would travel back to the twenty-first century, that I'd need to make a choice between Alexander and my old life.

A sudden rap at the door jerks me from my thoughts. My hands freeze on the broom handle. For a moment, I hold my breath, listening. Footsteps scrape against the porch, slow, deliberate, circling the house. Panic curls within me.

I can't be seen. I can't be caught.

I creep toward the window, tilting my head to peer through the curtain. And then I see her–Elizabeth Booth, peeking through the front window.

My stomach drops as she walks around the side of the house, muttering to herself aloud. "If I could get inside, tidy up for him... he needs a wife, a woman to care for him." Her words, soft at first, grow more fervent as she circles Alexander's house, her eyes scanning the inside of the house at every window.

I freeze, my knuckles white against the windowsill, holding my breath while silently praying she doesn't see me, but just then her head snaps up, and our eyes lock.

My heart stops, and Elizabeth screams a high-pitched, frantic sound. I stumble backward in utter shock.

"You're done for!" she shrieks, pointing a trembling finger at me. Her voice rises, brittle and furious. "Your life is over! Do you hear me? OVER!"

Elizabeth storms off down the path, screaming over her shoulder, "You will go straight to Beelzebub himself for this! Mark my words, Lila Bennett!"

Minutes pass. I pace the kitchen, the broom forgotten against the wall, every creak of the floorboards outside making me feel like I might faint. My hands won't stop shaking. She's gone to fetch them— I know it. Any moment now, the whole town will be at the door.

I think of running, but where would I go? I have nowhere to turn, nowhere to hide. Even the thought makes my stomach sink. All I can do is wait.

When the voices rise, I know Elizabeth has reached the village. I hear shouting, her voice carrying across the front yard: "Witch! Seductress! She bewitched Alexander!"

I stay low, looking out the window, careful not to be seen. The door stays locked, keeping them out, but not for long.

The pounding of boots on the porch makes me flinch. Then I hear Alexander's voice cutting through the chaos. "Stop! Leave my property at once!"

I hear Hezekiah shouting as well. "She is no witch! She has done nothing wrong! You are all a bunch of sheep! Stop this madness before every one of us hangs from the gallows!"

The villagers surge forward, caught up in Elizabeth's screams. The door rattles under their hands, then splinters as someone forces it open. I stumble back, my heart hammering, but there's nowhere to run. Hands grab at my arms, dragging me toward the street. I struggle, panic rising, but I am outnumbered, powerless. The crowd presses around me–voices shouting, pointing, accusing.

Elizabeth's face is a mask of triumph as she points at me, shrieking, "She's a seductress! A temptress! I saw her dance around the fire at night on the full moon! That's how she got Alexander to be with her!"

"No! I haven't done anything! I swear it!" I scream, struggling against the rough hands. Elizabeth points at me like a general directing an army, her face twisted with fury.

Another constable grabs Alexander. "And you!" one bellows. "Harboring a witch! Sharing a bed with a harlot who's not your wife! You are complicit!"

The crowd is alive with shouts, pointing fingers, and the ringing of voices chanting accusations. Alexander calls my name, but there is no escape. Elizabeth has brought the village into her frenzy, and now they drag us down the street to lock us up.

The iron door slams behind me, and the echo rattles my skull. The stench of damp stone, unwashed bodies, and fear fills my lungs. I stagger forward, gripping the wall for balance.

A figure lifts her head from the corner, her eyes weary. "I'm Mary Parker."

I swallow, my throat tight, and manage to force out, "Lila... Lila Bennett." My voice sounds small, fragile against the stone walls. She nods faintly, and I notice the tremor in her hands and the tension in her shoulders.

I sink to the floor, my knees pressed to my chest, shivering despite the heat. Every shadow twists like a threat. Every drip of water, every echoing footstep from the hall outside, makes me flinch. The walls press in, cold and unforgiving, as if they can reach inside me and squeeze.

I think of Alexander, and my chest tightens. I can almost see his face, twisted in disbelief and rage, and the pang of helplessness nearly crushes me. I can't call out to him. I can't move. I am trapped.

The stone bites into my spine and legs. My mind spins with visions of the noose, of the gallows, of Salem's whispers filling my ears. Elizabeth's shrill accusations cut through my memory, and I shiver violently at the thought.

I sit on the cold stone floor. The cell is dark, the door heavy and locked. There's no one coming to help me. No escape. No hiding. I press my back against the wall, forcing myself to breathe. I have to think. I have to plan. If I want to survive Salem, if I want to live, I can't wait for someone else to save me.

I will have to find my own way out of this.

LOVE POTIONS

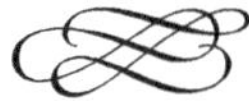

ALEXANDER

THE COURTROOM IS PACKED, voices of townsfolk and magistrates filling the room like a low, oppressive tide. I sit in the corner, my hands bound. My legs are restless, and every nerve is on edge. I search the gallery, looking for my father, mother, Phineas, and Hezekiah. Relief floods me when I see them, though the thought of being sentenced to death in front of my family makes my stomach churn.

The magistrate clears his throat, calling the room to order. My pulse hammers as Lila is brought forward, her hands chained but her head held high. She meets my gaze for the briefest second, and I see a fire in her eyes. She exudes defiance, strategy, determination, and it sends a charge of hope through me.

"Mistress Lila Bennett, you have been accused of witchcraft. How do you plead?"

Lila takes a deep breath. "I plead guilty, sir. I am a witch," she announces, her voice clear and unwavering. A hush drops over the room. "I cast a spell over Alexander Paine. That is why he let me into his home, why he shared his life with me, why he trusted me. He has done nothing wrong. Every choice he made was under the influence of my dark magic and love potions."

Gasps erupt across the courtroom. I glance at my father, his jaw tight, while my mother covers her mouth, her eyes filled with fear. Phineas fidgets, trying to look brave, while Hezekiah's expression turns to sheer curiosity, undoubtedly wondering what Lila has up her sleeve.

The magistrate leans forward. "And you claim, then, that this man is innocent?" he asks.

"Aye," she says without hesitation. "He acted as any man would under the influence I placed upon him. He is blameless. Let him go. If you are to punish anyone, punish me, but leave him free."

There's a pause so long it makes my ears ring. Then murmurs ripple through the crowd. A few nod in cautious agreement, while others frown, muttering under their breath. Lila's courage has me falling in love with her all over again.

"Is Mr. Paine still under your control?" the magistrate growls.

"Of course not," she replies. "The second you placed me in custody, my powers faded away. That is why I didn't use them to free myself. That is what happened with all the other witches, isn't it? The second you arrested them, their powers no longer worked, and that is how they were unable to save themselves. The same thing happened to me, and I can no longer control Alexander."

The magistrates look at each other, confused. They convene among themselves for what seems like hours.

I marvel at Lila's shrewd ability to use their own ignorance against them. Last month when Martha Carrier was on trial, they labeled her the "Queen of Hell" due to her indignant and stubborn tenacity. I shudder to think of what they'll call Lila.

Finally, the magistrate exhales, glancing at his colleagues. "Very well. Alexander Paine is to be released immediately. Lila Bennett will remain in custody for an additional day, while we consider the testimony and determine the extent of her… powers."

Relief crashes over me in a wave so sudden it nearly leaves me breathless. Lila catches my eye again, a fleeting, triumphant smile. Even behind the chains, she is commanding, fearless.

Hezekiah steps forward, muttering to the constables to release me.

My father's hand lands on my shoulder, solid and grounding. My mother's eyes glisten, but she manages a small smile. Phineas stumbles a little as he hugs me, still unsure how to navigate the chaos.

I glance back at Lila one last time as the constable escorts her back to her cell, and silently vow to rescue her just as she did me.

The walk from the courthouse feels unreal, as though the sun is too bright and the air too warm. I move almost mechanically, flanked by Hezekiah and Phineas, my parents falling into step behind us. My mind spins with everything Lila said and did, the shock still fresh.

We step through the front door of my parent's house, and the familiar scent of polished wood and home-cooked meals wraps around me like a small comfort. My mother's eyes are sharp as she studies me.

"Alexander," she says slowly. "Tell us the truth. Was she really a witch? Did she—did she put a spell on you?"

I shake my head, a small, incredulous smile tugging at my lips. "Of course not, Mother. That's… foolish. She said what she needed to say to get me released, nothing more. I swear it."

Father leans against the table, his arms crossed, nodding slowly. "She seems very clever. Loyal too, by the sound of it. You'd be foolish to let a girl like that slip away."

I chuckle softly, shaking my head. "You don't even know half of it."

Phineas grins, elbowing me lightly. "You better hold onto her, brother. Someone like that doesn't come along twice."

"I intend to," I say.

"Father, Mother." I take a deep breath. "I have decided to sell my land to Hezekiah and move to Boston with Lila."

"I think that's for the best, Son," Father says.

Mother's eyes are filled with tears as she asks, "Do you think they'll release Lila?"

"I'll do whatever it takes to save her, Mother, but please, no one speak a word of this to anyone."

Hezekiah and I sit at the rough pine table in my parents' study, quills in hand and ink pots nearby. We've already spoken of the terms, agreed on the sum, the boundaries, the livestock, and the rights to the land. Now it's just a matter of putting it down on paper.

"This is standard," Hezekiah murmurs, dipping his quill carefully. "We list the property, the buildings, the land, the livestock. I pay you, and you relinquish all claim."

I nod, already thinking of the work ahead at the farm–packing, moving, and saying goodbye to the place I've called home. The quill scratches against the parchment as we write, each word deliberate.

When the signatures are finished, Hezekiah hands me a leather pouch heavy with coins. The weight in my hand is real, tangible, a marker of what I've earned and what I've left behind.

We rise, shaking hands over the table. The gesture is more than formal. It's a recognition of years of friendship, of shared work and trust. "Thank you," I say, my voice low. "For everything."

He claps me on the shoulder. "Don't mention it, brother. You'll make your new start just fine."

When it's time to say goodbye, I turn to my parents first. Mother's eyes glisten as she reaches for my hands. "Alexander... you're leaving us," she says softly, her voice trembling.

"I am," I reply, trying to keep it steady. "But I'll visit someday soon. I promise."

Father steps closer, placing a hand on my shoulder. "You've made the right choice. Be sure to keep your heart strong, son. And remember, you always have a home here."

Phineas shifts nervously. "I'm going to miss you, brother."

"I'm going to miss you too," I answer, hugging him tight. "More than I can say."

Mother pulls me into a long embrace, holding me close. "Be safe, Alexander."

"I will, Mother," I whisper.

Father clasps my shoulder firmly. "We'll be waiting for your letters, and we'll pray for your journey. Take care of yourself."

I nod, swallowing hard. "I will. I promise."

Phineas gives a small, awkward grin. "Write when you can, and don't get into any more trouble."

"I'll do my best," I say, trying to smile despite the lump in my throat.

Hez and I leave my parents' house, the late morning sun bright overhead. I lead him down the path to my property, the familiar creak of the gate sounding different today, more final somehow. My chest tightens as I take in the farmhouse, the barn, the animals stirring in the yard.

Inside, I move from room to room, gathering belongings and placing them into the wagon: tools, blankets, personal items, anything I'll need for the next chapter. Each object carries memories, each corner a story.

I grab my axe from the barn and pause, running my hands over the stall doors, whispering soft goodbyes to the animals I've raised since birth. I murmur farewells, my voice thick with emotion.

I grip Hezekiah's shoulder. "I don't know when we'll see each other again."

He shakes his head, his jaw tight. "We will see each other soon enough. I'll visit you in the city. You'll be fine, Alexander. Just promise me you'll take care of yourself, and Lila."

"I will," I say, my voice low. "And you—watch out for Phineas. Keep him out of trouble."

He laughs. "You have my word. I'll haunt him for the rest of my days."

We clasp hands, holding the grip a beat longer than usual. Years of friendship, of scraped knees, boyhood hunting trips, sneaking out at night to go fishing, and shared work pass between us in that simple gesture.

"I'll miss you," I admit.

"Same here," he says. "More than I can say, but you've got your path now."

I hook my mare to the wagon, checking the harness one last time. Satisfied, I climb up onto the driver's seat, reins in hand.

I wave to Hez as I drive away, the wagon creaking. I urge the mare forward, and the path beneath us narrows, lined by the shadows of the trees. I drive out into the woods, the familiar sights of home falling away behind me.

I ease the wagon to a stop in a small clearing, the trees pressing in around me. Darkness gathers, the forest swallowing the edges of the world. I grip the reins loosely, my mare stamping softly on the ground. I'll wait here until nightfall, and then I'll make my way back to Lila.

FOXGLOVE

LILA

THE STONE FLOOR steals every drop of warmth from me. This time they've tossed me into a cell by myself. I sit in the shadows, listening to the guards' boots echo faintly down the hall then fade into silence. The night is humid, and though I'm exhausted, sleep won't come.

A whisper cuts through the stillness. "Lila."

I rush to the narrow window. Moonlight falls in pale stripes across Alexander's face, close enough to touch if not for the iron between us. His expression is taut with worry, his hands clenched tight around the cold metal.

"Alexander," I breathe, relief crashing over me. "You came."

"I'll get you out," he says fiercely. "No matter what it takes."

I grip the bars until they bite into my palms. He means every word, but brute force won't win against chains and iron bars. I lean closer, my voice low. "Then listen. I have a plan."

His eyes fix on mine, desperate, waiting.

"You have to go to Miriam," I whisper. "Ask her for foxglove."

His brow furrows. "Foxglove? That's poison, Lila."

"Only in the wrong dose," I tell him quickly. "I'll take just enough to slow my pulse until no one can find it. At dawn, when the guards come, they'll think I've died in the night. They'll wrap me in a sheet and carry me out."

He stares at me, horrified. "So they'll believe you're dead?"

"Yes. Please, Alexander. You have to trust me. This is the only way out." I press my hand through the bars until my fingers brush his. "I won't really be gone. The foxglove will only put me in a deep dream-like state, the kind that feels like sleep without end. My body will be still, my breath faint, my pulse impossible to feel, but I'll be alive. You'll come for me, as if to bury me, and instead you'll take me away."

His jaw works, torn between fear and hope. "And you're sure you'll wake? What if you take too much?"

"I will wake up," I whisper. "By the time you have me out of this place, I'll wake. You just have to trust me, Alexander."

For a long moment, he says nothing. Then he nods once, sharply. "I'll go. I'll get it."

He presses his forehead to the bars, and I lean close, so the cold iron is all that separates us. Then he's gone, swallowed by the night.

I pace the length of the cell, clutching the memory of his promise like a flame against the dark. At last, the sound of soft footsteps draws me back to the window.

"Lila."

He's there, breathless, and in his hand a small bundle. He slips it through the bars, and our fingers brush as I take it. Foxglove. My freedom.

"Just before dawn," I whisper, holding it to my chest. "I'll take it, and they'll think I'm gone. Don't be afraid when you see me. I'll only be asleep, waiting for you."

His hands grip the bars so hard they tremble. "Lila, I love you."

"I love you," I breathe, my heart breaking and burning all at once. "And I'll see you when the night is over."

Alexander vanishes into the dark, and the hours drag like centuries. I sit pressed against the cold wall of my cell, the bundle of foxglove clutched in both hands. Every sound seems louder now—the drip of water in some far-off corner, and the restless scratching of mice in the straw. I wait, counting my breaths, watching for the first pale gold of morning to seep through the slit of my window.

When at last the darkness softens, my chest tightens. It's time.

My fingers tremble as I unwrap the bundle. The sharp, bitter scent fills my nose, metallic and earthy. I break up the herb, remembering Alexander's warning look, and press the rough leaves to my lips. The taste is worse than I imagined: acrid, burning, and clinging to my tongue like ash. I have to force myself to swallow.

Heat rushes to my head almost at once, spinning my vision. The cell tilts, sways, then steadies in strange silence. My pulse slows. My arms feel heavy, like I'm sinking into the stone itself. I fight the instinct to resist, to cling to wakefulness. This is what I planned, what I asked for.

The dizziness swallows me whole.

And then I'm freezing cold.

I jolt awake with a gasp. My body is flat against hard pavement, icy air stinging my lungs. I blink up into darkness, and realize I'm back in the empty parking lot. Street lights buzz overhead, the same ones that flickered the night I slipped and fell. The ground glitters faintly with ice, the breath leaving my mouth in frosted clouds.

My heart slams in my chest as I push myself upright, numb fingers digging into the slick ground. My car is only a few feet away, coated in frost, just as it was before. The driver's side window is fogged from the inside. A thin crust of snow clings to the hood, and clenched in my hand is the foxglove–the same leaves, the same bitter-sweet poison. Proof it wasn't a dream.

I stagger to my feet, wrapping my arms around myself. The parking lot is silent except for the low hum of a nearby streetlight–no voices, no horses, no smoke rising from chimneys, only the hum of modern life pressing in all around me.

I fumble for my keys, finding them a few feet away from where I fell, unlock the car, and slide into the seat. The cold bites through my coat as I grip the wheel. If I turn the ignition, if I drive away, I could go home, home to heat and safety and the familiar. I could tell myself that my time in the seventeenth century was just some strange nightmare, that none of it was real.

Memories of Alexander flood me: our first meeting in the market, tall and handsome, buying a cookie for little Caitie. The way he never hesitated to help Miriam and me when we asked him to help us save baby Mercy. His refusal to give up even when danger loomed. Every small act, every brave choice, every time he kissed me, every time he whispered my name… it all comes back now, weaving together the man I've come to love, the one I can't imagine leaving behind.

A sob breaks from my lips, sharp and guttural. I can't abandon Alexander. I clutch the foxglove.

Love is a choice.

I sit in the driver's seat, tears streaming down my cheeks. This car is mine, this *world* is mine, and everything I ever thought I wanted waits for me here: school, a career, friends who know me by name, and no one accuses me of anything that could get me sent to the gallows. I have a future here that makes sense.

And yet, I choose him. I will always choose him.

With shaking hands, I lift the remaining foxglove to my mouth. The bitter taste burns down my throat, sharper than before, and my body seizes with nausea. My vision blurs, my heartbeat slows, and then there's nothing but black.

When I start to wake, the first thing I notice is the suffocating pressure, cloth presses against my mouth, my nose, my eyes–a sheet. It wraps around my head so tightly I can barely pull in a breath. The air is stiflingly hot and heavy. Panic claws at me, but my limbs won't respond. I'm alive, but only just barely.

Rough hands lift me. My body rocks with each step as guards carry me like a sack of grain. Voices mutter above me, muffled through the fabric.

"This one's dead. Good riddance," one says.

"Best to drop her outside," another replies. "Some poor soul will dig the hole later."

The sheet smothers the sound of their laughter as they let me fall. My back hits the ground, jarring the air from my lungs. I fight the urge to gasp, to move, to give myself away. Instead I lie still, and for a moment, I wonder if I've gone too far, if the foxglove has dragged me halfway to the grave already.

Their footsteps fade.

Silence.

Then—footsteps again. Lighter. Quicker. A voice I'd know anywhere, ragged with relief.

"Lila."

Strong arms gather me up. The sheet pulls loose, light spilling over my face. My first deep breath scorches my chest, but it's air. I blink through the haze until his face comes into focus–Alexander, his eyes shining, his jaw trembling as he looks at me.

"Let's get out of here," I whisper, my voice barely a thread.

Without another word, he lifts me higher in his arms and carries me toward the shelter of the woods. The prison, the guards, and the danger fall away behind us. All that matters is the rhythm of his heart against my ear and the safety of the dark trees closing around us.

Alexander carries me deeper into the woods until we reach his wagon. He lowers me gently to the ground. My body still feels weak, my head heavy.

He turns to help me into the wagon, but then he hesitates. His hand lingers at the edge of the seat, his eyes burning with something he can't seem to hold back.

"Wait," he says. His voice trembles, and for once it's not with fear but with something larger, stronger. He steps in front of me, takes both my hands, and sinks down onto one knee in the dirt.

I gasp. "Alexander…."

He looks up at me, his eyes shining in the thin wash of dawn light. "I nearly lost you. Watching them chain you, listening to them speak of your death… I can't bear it." His grip on my hands tightens. "Lila, I don't know what tomorrow brings, or what Boston holds, but I know I can't face a day without you. Be my wife. Choose me, as I have chosen you, for all the days God grants us."

Tears sting my eyes as I sink to my knees in front of him, our foreheads nearly touching. "Yes," I whisper, my voice breaking.

His relief is so fierce it almost knocks him backward. He laughs, half-choked, pulling me against him, kissing my hands, my face. I feel whole. I have chosen my path, and it is him.

He helps me stand again with a tenderness that makes my chest ache. "Then it's settled," he says softly, brushing a tear from my cheek. "We'll make it official when we get to the city."

We climb into the wagon together, side by side. His mare stamps the ground, restless, as if even she knows it's time to leave Salem behind. Alexander takes up the reins, and with a flick of his wrist, the wheels begin to turn.

The road ahead is uncertain, but my choice is not. I am no longer a woman caught between centuries. I am Alexander's fiancée, and together we drive toward Boston, into our future.

In the fadeout of the song *Rhiannon,* one of the most powerful witches of all time talks about love being a state of mind. And I think she's onto something there. Love is a choice you make every day, even when the world seems determined to pull you apart.

BOSTON

ALEXANDER

THE WHEELS of the wagon creak as the forest thins the closer we get to Boston. I glance at Lila, seated beside me, clutching the bundle of blankets I brought along. Her hair tumbles loose across her shoulders. Bonnets are unnecessary now. For a second, I nearly panic at the thought of losing her again.

"Lila," I murmur, my voice low, hesitant. "What if… what if Miriam's warning comes true? What if you're faced with the choice again between staying here, or going back?"

She tilts her head. "Alexander," she says softly. "I faced that choice the moment I took the foxglove. I passed out and went back to my time. I had the rest of it in my hand, and I weighed my options. Every dream, every future I could have… it was you, here, waiting for me." Her eyes meet mine, shining. "And I chose you."

Relief crashes through me like an ocean wave. I don't even think. I just lean forward, capturing her face in my hands, tilting her chin up. My lips find hers, pressing hard, desperate, tasting the fear and the promise and the impossible relief all at once.

When I finally pull back, just enough to look into her eyes, I can't keep the laugh of disbelief from escaping me. "You chose me," I whisper, my voice thick.

"I did," she says, a smile breaking through the tension. "I always will."

And in that moment, the future is ours. Whatever our new life in the city holds, I know we'll face it all together.

THE STREETS OF BOSTON BUZZ AS OUR WAGON WHEELS CLATTER OVER the cobblestones. I keep my eyes on the familiar landmarks, but Lila's hand in mine reminds me why none of this feels ordinary. We're nearly strangers in this city, yet together, we feel invincible.

Our first night is at a modest inn, its small rooms smelling of smoke and fresh linens. Lila settles herself near the window, tracing her fingers over the sill, her eyes distant. "It's strange," she whispers. "Boston is nothing like it is in my time, and yet, I still feel more at home here than anywhere."

I squeeze her hand. "I feel the same way."

The next morning, we begin our search for a house. Every turn brings new streets lined with brick and clapboard homes, each with possibilities and pitfalls. Some are cramped, barely enough room for us and our belongings. Others are grand but cold, impersonal. I see the worry in Lila's eyes each time we step into another foyer, imagining her trying to make it feel like home.

"This one," she says suddenly, pointing to a two-story brick house with wide windows and a large garden. The door creaks open to reveal a sunlit parlor, wooden beams above, and fireplaces that promise warmth. She runs her hands along the mantle, then glances at me with a smile I've memorized. "I can see us here."

I nod, relief washing over me. The money Hezekiah gave me for my farm rests in my pocket. We meet with the seller, agree on terms, and before long, the papers are signed, and the house is ours. I feel a weight lift. The past with all its shadows stays behind in Salem, replaced with this promise of life and safety.

The next few days are a whirlwind of unpacking, shopping, and arranging. Lila's decorative touch is everywhere: as she picks out curtains to catch the morning light just so, places herbs and flowers in every room, and sets the hearth with care. I watch her move through the rooms, transforming space into home, heart and warmth radiating from every gesture.

That evening, I sit at the small desk near the kitchen window, pen in hand. I write to my parents, telling them we are secure and happy, that Lila and I are together, and that our new home is more than I could have hoped. I don't mention Lila by name, of course, but they will understand.

I glance across the room at my beautiful wife-to-be, arranging a vase of white roses. She catches my eye and smiles. Here, together, we have created something sacred: love, safety, and a life that belongs only to us.

I rise, crossing to her side, and brush a strand of hair from her face. "We've made it," I whisper, more to myself than to her.

Boston is no longer just a city. It's ours, and for the first time in a long while, I believe that what we have together is enough to endure anything.

THE MORNING SMELLS OF RICH SOIL AND FRESH VEGETABLES AS WE STEP off the worn cobblestones into the small market garden behind the Boston market, a job I secured through a cousin of Hezekiah's who owns the city's finest greenhouses. Lila and I are tending their plots now, growing lettuces, cabbages, and herbs for local kitchens and market stalls, and my hands ache pleasantly from hauling crates, turning soil, and carefully nurturing the young plants. There's a satisfaction here I hadn't expected in a city in the quiet rhythm of work that feels familiar.

I run my fingers over the leaves of basil, inhaling its peppery scent, and a grin spreads across my face. This is work I know, work I can see the results of. I've traded the wide fields of Salem for a handful of city garden plots, but the satisfaction is no different. The sun warms my back as I dig out weeds and straighten rows of potted plants.

A young boy passes, carrying a basket of radishes. "Mr. Paine," he calls, tipping his cap. "The first carts of your lettuce are selling fast at the market."

I nod, pleased. "Good work, lad."

Lila strolls up behind me, her skirts brushing the soil, her hands full of wildflower seeds she insists on planting along the edges of the beds. She smiles, watching me wipe sweat from my brow. "You love this job, don't you?"

I glance at her, catching the sparkle of amusement in her eyes. "I do. It's honest work. I can see what I've done at the end of the day. And the city... it's not so bad when you can bring a little green into it."

She kneels beside a row of thyme, planting her flowers with careful hands. "It's perfect. I think we could even expand this plot."

I grin, wiping my hands on my trousers. "Exactly, and you know the best part? They let me bring this exquisitely attractive lady to help me every day."

She reaches up, brushing a smudge of dirt from my cheek. "I'm glad you're happy," she murmurs, leaning close. "And we'll make this place ours, just like the house. Boston can be ours if we work for it."

I pull her close, inhaling the scent of lavender and her hair mingling together, and I feel contentment, hard-earned and true. The chaos of Salem feels like a lifetime ago. Here, we grow food, we grow roots, and most importantly, we are growing a life together.

I glance down the rows at the tiny green shoots reaching toward the sun, and I know I'm exactly where I'm meant to be. The city is alive around us—market shouts, horse hooves, and chatter—but in this small patch of earth, Lila and I have carved our own little world.

Late in our first month in Boston, a small envelope arrives by courier. I break the wax seal with a careful twist of my fingers. My father's familiar hand curls across the page, his words looping in steady, sure script. My stomach tightens as I read.

Father, Mother, and Phineas are alive and well, even still cheerful in small ways. Relief floods me, but it is tempered by the rest of the letter. Salem is still in the throngs of madness. Women are being hanged for accusations whispered in the dark, and now a few men, too, have met the gallows. Fear and hysteria continue to choke the town, unchecked and brutal.

I set the letter down, rubbing my eyes, trying to shake the sadness. Lila leans against the doorway, curiosity written across her face. "Alexander?"

"Salem," I murmur, my voice tight. "It hasn't stopped. They're still killing them. Even some men have been hanged now."

Her hand finds mine. "We left all that evil behind, and yet it's still out there, tearing people apart." Her thumb strokes the back of my hand. "I'm so glad we moved to Boston."

I nod, letting a small breath escape. "It's different here. One can see it at a glance–the markets, shops, the smells of bread and roasted meats, the clamor of business, the hum of people living without fear of being accused at every turn. There's life in every street. In Salem, it was always whispers, shadows, suspicion. Here… life feels alive."

She smiles, lifting a small bouquet of herbs from the windowsill. "And yet we brought a little of the woods with us," she teases, placing them on the table.

I laugh, shaking my head. "You're right. You've made this place ours already."

I pull Lila close, resting my chin on the top of her head as we listen to the city stirring beyond our windows. For once, there is no fear, no rush, no shadow of the past pressing in, just us and our happy home.

MAGICAL

LILA

MIRIAM STANDS BEFORE ME, adjusting the laces of my gown. The fabric, once a stark white, now carries the soft blush of a rose garden in full bloom. A week ago, I sent for her, knowing she would understand the importance of this day and the significance of the gown.

"We've done well," Miriam says, her voice a whisper of approval.

I nod, my fingers brushing the full skirt. The pink hue is subtle, achieved through the careful soaking application of madder root and safflower petals. The gown clings to my form, its bodice embroidered with intricate floral patterns, a testament to the hours spent in its creation. The embroidery soaked up more of the dye, causing it to be more of an eye-catching vibrant coral tone. The sleeves billow slightly at the wrists, gathered with delicate lace.

Miriam steps back, her gaze appraising. "You look radiant."

I smile. "I never imagined I'd be standing here, in a gown like this, in a time so different from my own."

She meets my eyes, understanding passing between us. "Yet, here you are, right where you belong."

I turn to the mirror, taking in the reflection of a woman poised to marry the man of her dreams, in a world that once felt foreign but now feels like home.

The garden smells of early autumn and crisp earth, sunlight sifting through the branches. I clutch the bouquet of delicate amber petals in my hands and take a slow, calming breath. The wooden arch is draped with ivy and clusters of pale flowers, and the small gathering of friends and family waits just beyond the edge of the lawn. Their faces are bright, warm, expectant. Somehow, I can't quite believe this is real. That I'm standing here, in the center of a brand new Boston, in the 1600s, about to marry the man I love.

Alexander stands at the end of the aisle, his hands folded, his eyes fixed on me. Even from here, I can see a thrill in his expression, of something barely contained. My chest tightens, a sweet ache I've known since the first moment I realized I loved him.

Miriam stands beside me, her eyes gleaming with pride. She's my anchor today, steady and certain, and I know I couldn't have imagined anyone else at my side. Hezekiah is near Alexander, his shoulders squared, the picture of calm, best man, best friend.

Alexander's parents and Phineas are here, their faces filled with pride and happiness. I catch a glimpse of his father, his hands clasped behind his back, his eyes brimming with reverence. His mother's smile is beautiful, and Phineas waves at me subtly. I wave back.

Mary, Rebecca Nurse's daughter, stands with her husband and little Caitie, who clutches a basket of goldenrod petals. Their presence is a living thread connecting me to this place, this time. Somehow, despite everything, life goes on here too, and I feel honored to be part of it.

I step forward, the whisper of my gown the only sound. When I reach Alexander at the arch, the minister's voice rises gently over the hush, solemn and steady as he leads us through the vows. The words themselves are familiar, ancient promises woven into the fabric of countless unions before ours, yet today they feel as though they were spoken for us alone. My heart pounds, each syllable binding me more tightly to the man standing across from me.

Alexander's gaze never wavers. His hands are warm as they close over mine, his touch steady even as I feel my own fingers tremble. I murmur my vows, my voice carrying, and when he answers in turn, the strength and certainty in his tone steals my breath.

There is no hesitation. No shadow of doubt. Only us, and the life waiting ahead.

The minister pronounces us husband and wife, and Alexander draws me into his arms. The kiss is tender at first, then deepens with the weight of every promise we have just spoken aloud, sealing the moment not only in front of our gathered family and friends, but in the marrow of my soul.

Laughter and applause ripple through the garden as our lips part. For a moment, the world holds still, sunlight spilling golden through the trees, petals stirring on the breeze, the air alive with joy.

Simple elegance surrounds us: sunlight, flowers, joy, and the steady certainty that, no matter the century, love can carve its own home.

The clinking of glasses and the warm murmur of conversation wraps around us as the reception begins in a sunlit pavilion at the edge of the garden. Long tables are draped in soft linens, scattered with blossoms that mirror my bouquet.

I slip my hand into Miriam's as we move toward our seats, leaning in just enough that no one else notices. "Thank you," I whisper, my voice almost drowned out by the chatter around us. "For everything. You were right."

Her fingers tighten around mine, a faint smile curving her lips. "I knew you'd understand someday," she murmurs, her eyes flicking around as if to make sure no one is listening.

"I did," I continue, my cheeks warming. "I really did have a choice between going back to my own time or staying here with Alexander. And now I understand why you stayed, even when life in this century is harder. Sometimes it's not about ourselves. It's about being there for other people."

Her expression softens, and I feel the gravity of that shared knowledge between us, a secret bridge across time. "And I can see why," I add quietly. "Being here… it's beautiful. And I—"

I glance down at my pink dress and run a hand through my hair, loose across my back. "I love being able to wear colors, to wear my hair down, not a stiff bonnet. All the Puritan rules and constraints… they're stifling those people. That's why Salem fell apart. That's why it turned on itself."

"You'll have a much better life here in Boston," she says, her voice low. "You belong here now."

I nod, smiling, and turn just as Alexander rises to speak. He clears his throat, and the chatter dies down as all eyes turn toward him.

"My friends, my family," he begins. "Today I have the greatest honor of my life. Not just because I am marrying the woman I love, but because I have the privilege of sharing my life with someone who makes every day brighter, stronger, and more full of life than I could've ever dreamed. Lila, you are my heart, my future. I promise to care for you, to honor you, and to grow with you through every season, every challenge, and every joy this life will bring us."

A flush rises to my cheeks, and I feel tears prick my eyes. My chest swells with a warmth I've never known, with acceptance, love, and the wonder of belonging. The applause and cheers roll over me, but I barely notice. I only notice Alexander's hand in mine, his eyes shining with adoration.

I raise my glass, and Alexander meets my gaze, smiling. We dine, drink, and dance, laughter and music floating through the evening. Our wedding day is magical and perfect.

Eventually, the garden fades into twilight, lanterns glowing warm against the dusk, the sounds of these precious moments lingering like a melody I would never forget. When guests begin departing, Miriam clasps my hands one last time.

"It's time for me to return to your house," she says. "I'll watch over it while you're on your honeymoon. Travel safely, and I'll see you soon Mrs. Paine," she adds, causing a blush to bloom across my cheeks.

"Mrs. Paine," I giggle. "I do enjoy the sound of that. Thank you for being here on our most special day, Miriam."

"Of course, Lila. We witches must stick together," she says with a wink.

"You don't think *I'm* a witch, do you?" I laugh.

"Only if you want to be." Miriam shrugs, leans in, kisses my cheek, and vanishes into the evening fog to go house sit for us while we're gone.

Alexander and I slip away quietly, leaving Boston's narrow streets behind as a small cart carries us northwestward. The air grows crisper, tinged with pine and earth, and the sounds of the city give way to the rhythm of wheels over dirt.

By the time we reach Concord, the moon has risen high, casting silver light over rolling meadows and woods. The cabin waits on the edge of Walden Pond, simple but sturdy. Alexander helps me down, staring into my eyes as though he can't quite believe we are truly alone now, husband and wife.

"It's not much," he says softly, his gaze darting toward the cabin as though apologizing for its rough-hewn walls and narrow windows. "But it is quiet. I was able to rent it from the owner for about half the price of the inns in the city. You're sure this is where you want to stay the night?"

I squeeze his hand, a secret blooming in my chest. I asked for this place. Not just for its quiet, not just for its beauty, though it has both in abundance, but because I know what it will mean one day. Here, long after we are gone, a writer will build his cabin and pen words that will echo through centuries. *"I went to the woods because I wished to live deliberately..."* Henry David Thoreau's line beats in my mind, though it has yet to be written.

And here we are, living deliberately.

"It's perfect," I whisper.

The door creaks open beneath Alexander's hand, and a bed of fresh linens stands in one corner. He watches me with a reverence that steals my breath. "You are so astonishingly captivating," he murmurs.

I laugh lightly, loosening the flowers pinned in my hair until curls tumble free across my face. "That's just the wine talking," I say, standing before him.

"No," he says firmly, closing the space between us. His fingers brush mine. "It's the truth. I'm the most blessed man in the world."

Outside, the pond lies still beneath the moon, reflecting the stars in its glassy surface. Inside, I press my lips to Alexander's, breathing in his scent. "Take me, Mr. Paine," I whisper.

Alexander lifts me in his arms, my legs on either side of his waist, my wedding gown billowing around us, and kisses me deeply as though he'd been waiting for centuries to make me his wife. I moan into his lips, causing his lust to ignite the fire within him. He kisses my collarbone and finds my breasts through the fabric, squeezing them until I'm begging to be released from the laces.

I turn away from Alexander, and sweep my hair to the side so he can untie my dress. Instead, he pulls me flush against him and buries his mouth in my bare neck, causing me to shiver with excitement. He steps back just enough to untie my gown. As it falls to the floor, I step out of it and face him again.

I stand before him, cloaked only in the simplest and sheerest of undergarments. "Your turn, my love," I say.

Alexander obliges, undressing quickly, and I pull off my slip with lust-fueled urgency. He takes me in his arms and carries me to the bed, laying me down on my back while sucking my breast into his mouth, causing my back to arch in pure pleasure. His hand on my other breast, toying with my sensitive flesh in the most delicious way.

I reach down and stroke his thickness, feeling how ready he is for me, and becoming even more filled with desire. When he enters me, filling me up completely, I can't help but move with him, our hips bucking in perfect rhythm.

Moving my hands to his strong back, pulling him all the way into me as we become one, I feel the elation building until I shudder in pure rapturous bliss. Alexander trembles, the heat of his body and the tightening of his muscles telling me he has reached the same peak of release.

I close my eyes and let the stillness wrap around me, Alexander's hand in mine. Every choice, every risk, every step that brought me here feels right. For the first time, I am fully present, fully certain, and entirely at peace with the life I have chosen.

BELONGING

LILA

THE DAWN LIGHT creeps over Walden Pond, brushing the cabin in pale gold. Alexander moves quietly, gathering our few belongings, folding our blankets and packing our modest satchel. I follow his rhythm, tucking my extra clothes into a basket, savoring the stillness of the morning. Two days here have been a world apart, a bubble of peace and playfulness, and yet I can't shake the pull of Salem from my mind.

"Do you ever wonder," I begin cautiously, brushing crumbs from the breakfast table, "if we could help the people back in Salem? Not physically–I don't want to go back and be hanged–but with letters and words. With my knowledge of the law, maybe I could help."

Alexander pauses, looking up at me. His expression is calm, thoughtful. "You mean like influencing things from a distance?"

I nod, biting my lip. "Exactly. I can't stop the chaos in person, but maybe I could sway some minds, record things, maybe prevent more deaths. I keep thinking about everything I've seen, all the fear, the accusations. If there were a way…." My voice falters, the weight of it all pressing down on me.

He takes a long breath. "You know, my father mentioned something similar at our wedding reception. He was speaking of Increase Mather, and remembered something he'd said. 'It were better that ten

173

suspected witches should escape than one innocent person should be condemned.' He told me how that line helped shape the ministers' approach in Salem. It was one of the things that turned opinion against relying on spectral evidence. They're still holding many prisoners, but they haven't executed anyone since."

"So the magistrates do listen sometimes, and that means there could still be a way the trials could be steered toward fairness so the prisoners can be let go."

"Aye," he says gently, gathering my hand in his. "Increase Mather, and his son Cotton too… their voices made a difference. They didn't stop it all overnight, but they began to tilt the scale."

I lean against him, letting the warmth of his chest steady my racing thoughts. "I want to be part of that. Not in danger, not hanging over a scaffold, but using what I know: writing, law, reason."

Alexander smiles. "Then we'll begin as soon as we get home."

The wagon waits outside, its wheels creaking as we finish packing. Hand in hand, we step into the growing light, ready for the next part of our journey, but my mind is already racing ahead, sketching legal arguments, letters, and essays that might, somehow, save lives in a town that seems determined to destroy them.

The day stretches long before us as the cart lumbers eastward, leaving the quiet of Walden Pond behind. The sun is barely climbing when we set out, and by midmorning, the woods roll past in endless yellows and reds.

The journey is long. The roads are uneven and lined with the shadows of trees that seem to lean toward us as if curious. By late afternoon, the familiar shapes of the Naumkeag village appear over a rise, the smoke of cooking fires curling toward the sky. Relief and warmth bloom in my heart.

We are welcomed immediately with shouts of merriment and glee. Naya's mother approaches first, clutching her youngest child, while the woman who has been caring for baby Mercy carries the tiny infant in her arms. Mercy's little fingers curl around the fabric of her blanket, her wide eyes bright and curious. She's thriving, healthy, beautiful, and I can't help the tears that prick my eyes.

One of the men who speaks English steps forward, bowing slightly. "Welcome! What brings you to our part of the woods?" he asks.

I smile. "We have friends here. Naya is my friend, and we are celebrating. We just got married," I tell him proudly.

His eyes fill with wonder, and he laughs, clapping his hands together. He turns to the others, translating quickly, and the village bursts into movement. Someone retrieves Naya for me, and her beaming face brings me pure joy.

The elders invite us to stay, insisting that tonight is a night of jubilation, not rest. Bowls of food are set down, and Alexander is greeted warmly by the warriors, with questions and laughter spilling into the air. The fire is lit in the center of the village, flames dancing over faces bright with excitement. Music begins: drums, flutes, and sweet harmonious voices. Soon everyone is moving in circles, clapping, singing. I take Alexander's hand, and he smiles at me, his eyes reflecting the firelight.

We join the dance, our steps awkward at first, then in time with the rhythm. I glance around and see Mercy, swaddled and cooing, safe in the arms of her adoptive mother, the other children spinning around with delightful energy. Naya is the best dancer of them all.

In this moment, surrounded by life, music, and love, I feel a peace I have never known in a world that is alive and whole. Tonight, their village has become our home.

When daylight finds us, I hug Naya, and we each tell each other goodbye in our own way, perfecting a secret language all our own each time we meet. I will always consider her one of my greatest friends. We leave the Naumkeag village, the first pale light spilling across the forest as we travel southwest toward Boston.

By late evening, the familiar shapes of Boston rise over the horizon, and when we reach our street, Miriam on the porch, her shawl pulled around her shoulders. The moment she sees us, her eyes brighten. "Well, did you enjoy yourselves?" she calls, her tone light but curious.

Alexander grins, tipping his head toward me. "We did, Miriam. Truly."

I step down from the cart, brushing dirt from my skirts, and let her hands fall into mine. "It was magical and perfect," I add softly, glancing at Alexander. "The Naumkeag people welcomed us, and Mercy is thriving. It's astonishing, how full of life she is, even at just three months."

Miriam's eyes crinkle at the corners, and she laughs. "I'm glad to hear it. Now, tell me everything."

We settle at the small kitchen table, the smell of fresh bread and brewing tea filling the room. We recount our travels: the serenity of the cabin by the pond, the warmth of the Naumkeag people, and the festivities that stretched into the night. Then, naturally, our conversation turns to Salem.

"I can't stop thinking about it," I admit, tracing the rim of my teacup with a fingertip. "The fear, the accusations... the innocent people still at risk. I want to do something, using what I know of law, my writing, maybe even arguments that could sway those who listen."

Miriam nods, her eyes thoughtful. "Your words could help end it all, but you'd have to use an alias, of course. They'll never listen to a woman, especially when they presumed dead, whose body went missing."

"Of course. We'd use a pen name, but if we wrote and distributed enough letters to enough of the magistrates and people in charge, maybe we could get people released from those deplorable prison conditions."

Alexander reaches across the table, covering my hand with his. "Then we will, together. Here, now, with careful words and steadfast hearts."

The warmth of their confidence fills me, and for the first time since arriving in this century, I feel a clear path forming. I will act, not recklessly, but deliberately. And with Alexander and Miriam by my side, I know the voices of reason can echo where fear has taken hold.

I clear a space on the small wooden table, sunlight spilling across the worn surface, and lay out paper, ink, and quills. Alexander settles into the corner, keeping me company but leaving me the room I need. I take a slow, grounding breath, feeling the weight of history pressing gently on my shoulders. This is the moment I can act without risking my life. My mind races, recalling every trial I witnessed, every accusation, every shadow of fear that gripped the town.

I begin with a list: the names of the accused I know are innocent, the patterns of accusation, the testimonies that were twisted or misunderstood. Each line is a pulse of truth, a tether to reason I hope will reach Salem before more harm is done. Alexander leans over occasionally, suggesting ways to frame my words so they are firm yet measured, persuasive without inflaming the hysteria.

"I want them to listen," I murmur, dipping my quill in ink. "To see evidence, to recognize injustice, to reconsider reliance on spectral claims."

Alexander nods. "If anyone can show them reason, it's you. Your writing is precise, passionate, and true, just the right balance."

I begin drafting letters addressed to ministers who have sway in Massachusetts: thoughtful appeals urging fairness, citing laws and precedents, warning of the consequences of allowing fear to dictate justice.

Miriam brings tea, setting it beside me without interrupting, and I keep writing, the sun inching higher through the windows. I sketch charts, timelines, lists of witnesses whose voices were dismissed, and letters that could be sent by trusted messengers. The thought of Salem, the fear that grips it, the lives at stake, all pour onto the page.

I pause to read my words aloud, savoring their clarity, their reason, the logic that might break through the fog of panic. Alexander and Miriam listen, nodding, offering gentle suggestions. Together, we craft arguments that balance compassion and authority, appealing to the ministers' and magistrates' sense of duty as well as their conscience.

Finally, I lean back, my hand trembling from ink and effort, but the tension feels lighter. These pages are more than words. They are a shield for those who cannot defend themselves, a voice where terror has silenced reason. I glance at Alexander, who grins, his eyes shining with pride.

"We've done something today," Miriam says. "Even if it's just letters, you've begun the work of saving lives."

I nod. The task ahead is far from complete, but for the first time since arriving in this century, I feel the power of action. Salem may be shrouded in fear, but our voices will reach it. And perhaps, slowly, it will be enough to turn the tide.

A few days later, Miriam prepares to return to Salem, to care for the village as their healer once again. She rides in a small carriage, escorted by one of the Carter men who knows the roads well and will keep her safe along the journey.

Weeks pass after we send the letters. Alexander and I settle into our new rhythm in Boston, our mornings bright with sunlight and the smell of fresh produce in the greenhouses where he works, and I often visit to lend a hand.

Our evenings are full of conversation and laughter. For a time, I push Salem to the edges of my mind, focusing instead on the life Alexander and I are building together.

One afternoon, Alexander arrives with news that makes my heart leap. "The letters you wrote," he says, his eyes shining. "The ministers read them. The magistrates, too. They took them seriously enough to act."

I stop mid-step, gripping the counter, my chest tight with hope and disbelief. "What do you mean?"

"They began reviewing the prisoners immediately," Alexander says, his voice a mixture of awe and relief. "Every single person you listed, your careful notes, the evidence, the arguments, they acted on it. They're being released."

The words feel surreal, and I close my eyes, letting them sink in. Weeks ago, I had written in secrecy, signing each letter with a man's name used as a shield, so they would listen without prejudice.

I rush to the window, imagining the dark cells of Salem emptied one by one, the fear on innocent faces melting into stunned relief.

Tears prick my eyes, but they are the kind of tears that taste like triumph.

Alexander presses a kiss to my temple. "You did it, Lila. You saved them."

I turn to him, overwhelmed, with love and gratitude. "No. We did it together." I reach up, cupping his face.

For the first time in my life, I feel entirely secure. The girl who wandered through foster care, the girl who felt like an outcast, the girl who never quite fit in… she is gone. In her place stands someone who has found her purpose.

Alexander's hand in mine feels like the missing piece I didn't know I was searching for, and I understand now that every loss, every lonely night, every fear and uncertainty has led me to this moment. I was always meant to be here, in this time, with him, using my voice to save the innocent and bring justice where fear sought to rule.

The threads of my past, the chaos of Salem, and the love I have found converge into something whole, something enduring. I belong, truly, completely, and it is not just to Alexander, but to the world I can help shape, the people I can protect, the life I can finally call my own.

And in that belonging, in that knowing, I'm finally home.

ALSO BY ID JOHNSON

Stand Alone Titles

<u>All I Want for Christmas is Pooch</u>

(*sweet contemporary romance*)

<u>Christmas Memory</u>

(*sweet contemporary romance*)

<u>Meet Cute Me Under the Mistletoe</u>

(*sweet contemporary romance*)

<u>The Doll Maker's Daughter at Christmas</u>

(*clean romance/historical*)

<u>Pretty Little Monster</u>

(*young adult/suspense*)

<u>The Journey to Normal: Our Family's Life with Autism</u> (*nonfiction*)

<u>Found by the Alpha</u> (*fantasy romance*)

Sweet As Maple Syrup series

Leaving Autumn

Cold Turkey (coming Nov 1, 2025!)

Snowed Inn (coming Dec 1, 2025!)

Love Throughout Time

(*time travel romance*)

Back to Titanic

Back to Gettysburg

Back to Bunker Hill

Back to the Highlands

Back to Port Royal

Back to the Inquisition

Back to Salem

Back to Plymouth (Nov 2025)

Back to Whitechapel (Dec 2025)

Back to the Old West (Jan 2026)

Back to the Ton (Feb 2026)

Back to the Crown (March 2026)

Back to Pompeii (April 2026)

Silverwood Academy

(paranormal romance)

Vampire Hunter

World Builder

Realm Jumper

Celestial Springs

(psychological thriller/literary fiction/women's fiction)

Beneath the Inconstant Moon

The First Mrs. Edwards

Leaving Ginny

The Motherhood

(dystopian romance)

Rain's Rebellion

Rain's Run

Rain's Return

Ashes and Rose Petals

(contemporary romance/retelling of Romeo and Juliet and Cinderella)

Girl in the Attic

Girl From the Tomb

The Chronicles of Cassidy (based on The Clandestine Saga)

(young adult paranormal)

So You Think Your Sister's a Vampire Hunter?

Who Wants to Be a Vampire Hunter?

How Not to Be a Vampire Hunter

My Life As a Teenage Vampire Hunter

Vampire Hunting Isn't for Morons

Vampires Bite and Other Life Lessons

Gone Guardian

Death Does Not Become Her

Blood of the Vampire Hunter (based on The Clandestine Saga)

(paranormal romance)

Night Slayer

Shadow Stalker

Queen Catcher

Mother Hunter

Father Finder

Ghosts of Southampton series

(historical romance)

Prelude

Titanic

Residuum

Lusitania

Heartwarming Holidays Sweet Romance series

(Christian/clean romance)

Melody's Christmas

Christmas Cocoa

Winter Woods

Waiting On Love

Shamrock Hearts

A Blossoming Spring Romance

Firecracker!

Falling in Love

Thankful for You

Melody's Christmas Wedding

The New Year's Date

Charles Town Brides (based on Heartwarming Holidays Sweet Romance)

(Christian/clean romance)

From This Moment

Can't Help Falling in Love

It's Your Love

When You Say Nothing At All

My Girl

Unchained Melody

I Only Have Eyes For You

At Last

The Very Thought of You

Reaper's Hollow

(paranormal/urban fantasy)

Ruin's Lot

Ruin's Promise

Ruin's Legacy

When Kings Collide

(steamy historical romance)

Princess of Silence

<u>Princess of Hearts</u>

Collections

<u>Ghosts of Southampton Books 0-2</u>

<u>Reaper's Hollow Books 1-3</u>

<u>The Clandestine Saga Books 1-3</u>

<u>The Chronicles of Cassidy Books 1-4</u>

<u>Celestial Springs Collection</u>

<u>Heartwarming Holidays Sweet Romance Books 1-3</u>

<u>Heartwarming Holidays Sweet Romance Books 4-7</u>

Websites: https://idjohnsonwriter.com/

Follow us on TikTok: @roguewolfpublishing

Follow on Twitter @authoridjohnson

Find me on Facebook at <u>www.facebook.com/IDJohnsonAuthor</u>

Instagram: @authoridjohnson

Follow me on Bookbub: https://www.bookbub.com/authors/id-johnson